10/00

Mosby,

The Kennedy Center Cat

By Beppie Noyes

VSP Books

P.O. Box 17011, Alexandria, Virginia 22302

Other VSP Books About Very Special Places
Woodrow, the White House Mouse, by Peter and Cheryl Barnes
Marshall, the Courthouse Mouse, by Peter and Cheryl Barnes
House Mouse, Senate Mouse, by Peter and Cheryl Barnes
Capital Cooking with Woodrow and Friends, by Peter and Cheryl Barnes,
with Shelly Corini
Alexander, the Old Town Mouse, by Peter and Cheryl Barnes
Nat, Nat, the Nantucket Cat, by Peter and Cheryl Barnes, with Susan Arciero
Martha's Vineyard, by Peter and Cheryl Barnes, with Susan Arciero
Cornelius Vandermouse, the Pride of Newport, by Peter and Cheryl Barnes,
with Susan Arciero
Order these books through your local bookstore by title,
or order by calling 1-800-441-1949, or from our website at
www.VSPBooks.com
For a brochure and ordering information, write to
VSP Books, P.O. Box 17011, Alexandria, VA 22302

ISBN 0-9637688-8-3
Library of Congress Catalog Card Number: 98-075057
10 9 8 7 6 5 4 3
Printed in the United States of America

For Ceci

Contents

Welcome From the Author

Some people think that I made up the story of Mosby. Not so.

Years ago, while I was in Maine one summer, my friend, Ceci Carusi, called from Washington, D.C. She wanted me to write the story of a wild cat, a stray, she said, that was living in the Kennedy Center. At first I didn't believe her. I knew of that elegant marble building rising up beside the Potomac River called The John F. Kennedy Center for the Performing Arts. It had big theaters for plays, musicals and dance, and a main hall called "The Grand Foyer," which was one of the largest rooms in the world. It was certainly not a shelter for a stray cat! It didn't seem possible. But Ceci assured me it was true. She even brought him his cat food. She wanted me to write his story before something happened to him. So I did.

I spent many hours at the Center, talking to staff members who saw him, walking where he had prowled. I had to guess at some happenings and change a few characters. But Mosby did have many of these adventures. And Ed, the building manager, really never took a vacation—he didn't want to desert "his" cat! I went up to Mosby's Hideout in the unfinished theater and looked at his river view, watched the tourists trying to see through the dark glass and was amazed at Mosby's silent world.

I think I heard him, walking behind me somewhere in the shadows. But I never saw him.

I have had many cats before and since then. Peaches, Bess, Micmac and Mathew Vassar are watching me as I write this. They sit and purr in the sunlight on the window seat beside my desk. They are the latest four in a long parade of cats that have wandered through my life. But of all of them, I somehow love Mosby the most, even though I never saw him—or perhaps because I only saw him with my heart. Like many of the unnoticed and unknown, he had to be a courageous lover of freedom, a cat the founders of our nation would have been proud to hold—if he would have let them.

No one knows what really happened to this shadowy cat. One day, he simply disappeared. But he'd been such a ghostly creature that it was some time before anyone was really sure he was no longer there. So I wrote this story to give his life meaning and to please my friend, Ceci, who has such faith in me. She never doubted for a moment that I could write this book! Since it was first published 20 years ago, I have received many letters and calls about it from children of all ages, from cat lovers and first graders, teachers, grandfathers and young mothers, all of whom have found something important in the story of this strange and lonely cat.

I am not sure what it was they found. But I think my readers have sensed that Mosby is like their own true self, an independent spirit, a mysterious presence that seems to be just around the corner, sensed rather than seen. And like the man for whom the Center was named, he was gone before we knew him. And instead of me giving meaning to Mosby's life, I find that he has given meaning to my life, and, if you read this book, perhaps to your life as well.

I want to thank my publisher, Peter Barnes of VSP Books, for tracking me down in Maine and persuading me that he could republish this work. I want to thank Jaime Negron of the

Kennedy Center for being an enthusiastic supporter of dreams. I want to thank the Friends of the Kennedy Center, whose commitment to the creative life of Washington, D.C., and the nation is backed up by money and hard work. And I want to thank the volunteers and clerks in the Kennedy Center shops who remembered Mosby and my book and kept hoping that it would be reprinted. Finally, I wish to thank the spirits of wildness and independence that can live anywhere—in a big glass building in a busy city; down a dirty alley on a dead-end street; in a quiet place in the country; in an apartment building; in the White House; in the heart of this woman and in the story that I have written for a friend. And perhaps even in you, too.

BSN
Sorrento, Maine
September 1998

Preface

By Roger L. Stevens

Chairman, John F. Kennedy Center for the Performing Arts,
1961-1988

While the tale of the cat has been developing into a legend that is here recorded by Mrs. Noyes, I have been collecting over the years some fascinating stories told by actors who became acquainted with Mosby during performances at the Eisenhower Theater. For instance . . .

While Eugene O'Neill's great tragedy, "Long Day's Journey into Night," was being performed, Zoe Caldwell and her co-star Jason Robards frequently heard a sound that heightened the depressing atmosphere of the play in a way that couldn't have been anticipated by playwright, director or actors. In addition to the mournful cry of foghorns that helped establish the setting of O'Neill's boyhood home on Long Island Sound, wails not unlike keening at an Irish wake were heard as Mosby joined with the actors in performance.

Quite another impression was made on Barbara Bel Geddes as she starred in Jean Kerr's comedy, "Finishing Touches." Playing the sometimes-perplexed mother of a rambunctious family, the actress was at times further distracted by what sounded to her like the cries of a small baby. When "the baby" was heard off and on through more than one or two performances, she became sure it wasn't a sound coming from someone in the audience. She suspected the place was haunted until the histrionic instincts of Mosby were revealed to her.

IX

Audiences, too, sometimes became aware of the presence of Mosby, who would on occasion make use of a potent pause on stage to ad lib a line of his own—often with hilarious results.

Competition or no, Mosby gradually took on the status of house pet for the actors as well as the staff. As for the management, Mosby was one performer who never had to be paid.

Roger L. Stevens (1910-1998) was Chairman of the Board of Trustees of the John F. Kennedy Center for the Performing Arts from 1961, when he was appointed to build and run the then-National Cultural Center by President Kennedy, until 1988. He held that position through five presidential administrations. Mr. Stevens was Special Assistant to the President on the Arts from 1964 to 1968, and Chairman of the National Council on the Arts from 1964 to 1969. Having had a distinguished career as a theatrical producer and having specialized in real estate investments from coast to coast, Mr. Stevens used his talents to supervise the completion of the Center and to keep its three major auditoriums lighted throughout the year with artistic attractions of variety and excellence.

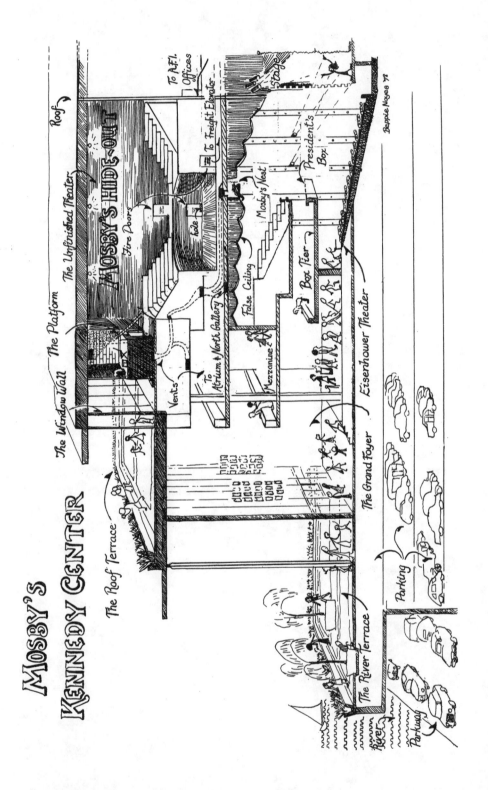

MOSBY'S
KENNEDY CENTER

Introduction

H is name was Mosby. He was big, gray and wild. He lived alone and liked it. He was a cat—a most unusual cat. Perhaps you may think there's nothing so unusual about a big, gray, wild cat living alone. But Mosby was unusual. He lived alone in the Kennedy Center—The John F. Kennedy Center for the Performing Arts—to give it its proper name.

The Kennedy Center is a great, white marble building beside the Potomac River in Washington, D.C.

It was built for plays and concerts, ballets and operas. There are entrance halls hung with flags of every state and every country. The main hall, called the Grand Foyer, is one of the biggest rooms in the world. It has red carpets and crystal chandeliers and walls of mirrors and glass. It is an elegant building.

Certainly not a place for a cat.

There are three theaters off this hall where people perform plays, music and dance. There is also a little theater where the American Film Institute (A.F.I., for short) shows all kinds of films. The A.F.I. offices are on the top floor, where some of our story takes place.

Down underground are acres of parking lots and more offices and back entrances where workers bring in scenery and band instruments and things like that. Around the building run marble balconies with trees and shrubs growing in them. On one side, the balconies look out on the river. On the other side, famous buildings of Washington peek through the trees.

Now, what kind of a cat would like to live in a place like that?

Mosby did.

On the top floor are a glamorous restaurant and a cafeteria, and there is an outdoor cafe on the balcony for nice weather. At the other end, past two halls called the Atrium and the North Gallery, is a tremendous room where they planned to build a "Little Theater." But the money ran out, so the builders left it unfinished. (It was finished years later.) That's where Mosby lived, in this dark, dusty, forgotten place, all by himself.

Hundreds of people came to the Kennedy Center day and night. People came to look at the building, watch the plays, listen to the music and see the films. People came to act in the plays, play music, dance and sing. People came to work in the offices and type and answer the phones and sell tickets. There were guides and guards and people selling postcards and souvenirs. There were cooks and waiters and waitresses to feed everyone. There were people to clean the Center and fix broken things.

There were committees helping raise money and organize and plan. There was Ed, who kept the building running—its manager. There was Roger, the head of everything—the "Chairman."

There were all these people. And there was Mosby, the cat.

He was the only soul living in the Kennedy Center all the time, day and night. So, in a way, it was his building.

This is his story. I've had to guess at some things and change a few characters around. But he really did have many of these adventures, and I've added nothing that couldn't have happened. So, here it is: the story of Mosby, the Cat who Lived in the Kennedy Center.

"He didn't play with the other kittens, but instead went off by
himself to watch his world."

1

Beginnings

There was a time when there was no Mosby and no Kennedy Center. Little brick houses stood side by side in the sun. Men, women and children lived in those houses. Rats and cats roamed the back alleys scrounging for food. That was a long time ago.

Then, one day, the people moved away, and great machines came and knocked down the houses, leaving piles of bricks and dust. They covered over the empty cellars. Weeds grew up where the houses had been. The rats ran fierce and hungry in the long grasses by the river.

Men came in shiny, hard hats. They put up a high fence around this empty land. They moved in trailers and built a big construction shed. They bent over blueprints and sighted through spyglasses and started to build a building.

As anyone living in a city knows, the rats can get out of hand when things are torn down. Cats came, attracted by the rats. Great fights waged unseen in the tall weeds. The builders welcomed the cats. In fact, Ed, the building manager, began feeding the cats to keep them around.

Some of the cats were tame ones, with perfectly good, warm homes to go back to. Others were the wild ones living in any city, roaming vacant lots and alleys, calling anywhere "home." Some of these found shelter and a safe hiding place in the building going up beside the river.

Mosby's mother was one of those who moved in. One spring night, in an empty carton, in a dark corner of the unfinished building, six kittens were born. Four were multicolored, one was white and one was gray. This last one was Mosby. He had a notch in one ear and a faint M on his forehead. He was different in other ways.

From the first, Mosby was independent. He didn't like to be held down. He squirmed and tried to escape his mother's paw when she washed his fur with her rough tongue. Some cats, like some people, simply don't like to be held.

As he grew stronger, he learned the kitten games of stalk, leap and pounce. He was clever; he was fast; he could make himself almost invisible. He didn't stay with the other kittens, but instead went off by himself to watch his world.

There were so many things to see. Mosby liked to watch the giant cranes lift a great steel beam, swinging it high against the clouds. The men in shiny hats would stretch out, pull it in, shouting and laughing, and settle it gently in the right place. Mosby liked to stalk the pigeons strutting on the crossbeams. He was too little to catch them yet, but he would crouch, motionless, watching them. Only the tip of his tail twitched and his teeth chattered as if he were cold.

Early each morning, in the deep darkness just before dawn, the mother cat rose and slipped out of the building to join the rest of the cats under the construction sheds. They came from everywhere, old cats, young cats, Persians, Siamese, sweet-

"He was surrounded by a sea of purring, growling, chirping
hungry cats."

faced Tabbies, and alley cats of every kind with scarred ears and greedy eyes.

At exactly the same time every morning, a car turned the corner, entered the gates and rolled to a stop. In the headlights sparkled a hundred eyes. As the driver got out, he was surrounded by a restless sea of purring, growling, chirping, hungry cats, tails high and eyes watching his every move. It was Ed.

Sometimes a shiny-hat would grumble, "I don't see why you bother with those grungy cats!"

Ed never answered. He just poured the food into an assortment of beat-up, old pans.

"Take it easy," he would say, his eyes sparkling through his glasses. "There's enough for all."

Mosby's mother started bringing home a few scraps or even a small bird or a mouse to feed her growing kittens, for they were beginning to need more than her milk. One morning, she decided she had waited on them long enough. It was time for the kittens to fetch their own food outside.

When she chirped to them, the other kittens followed her obediently. Not Mosby. He was independent. He danced around, stiff-legged and hid behind the box. His mother urged him with repeated mews, but Mosby ran off and pounced on his shadow.

So they left without him.

He watched them move off, in and out of the black shadows, across a beam silhouetted against the night sky. Mother cat looked back and called him, one last time, but he did not follow. They were gone, down a steep slanting board toward the ground far below. Mosby played chase-his-tail, then curled up in his box for a nap.

When he woke, the sun was up. They hadn't come back. Where were they? He was puzzled and hungry.

The shiny-hats were already at work. Rivet machines rat-a-tatted, cranes creaked, whistles shrieked, men shouted and

"Mother cat looked back and called him one last time."

laughed. But, somehow, Mosby didn't feel like watching. He went into his dark corner and tried to wash. It wasn't easy, this washing business! Every time he tried to reach the middle of his back with his tongue, he fell over. He soon fell asleep exhausted.

When the men stopped for lunch, Mosby crept out, looking for a snack. He stalked a delicious-smelling ham and cheese sandwich, but a worker saw him and—WHOP!—almost squashed Mosby with his shiny hat. Mosby ran back to his box to wait for the men to leave. He was hungry, but he had an ache deep inside that wasn't hunger. He heard a tiny kitten-cry. He jumped. His heart thumped. He looked around. There was no other kitten, only his own shadow.

"Mew."

There it was again. Suddenly Mosby realized it was his own voice he heard. It was embarrassing. Here he was, almost grown, and crying like a kitten. He curled his tail over his nose and tried to sleep.

When he awoke, it was almost dark; the building was silent; the men had left. He hurried to the place where he had last seen his mother and the other kittens. The wind whistled in the empty scaffold. He heard a rustle; his heart jumped. But it was only a piece of paper blowing. Mosby wandered the empty building, up and down, around corners, into unfamiliar places. He found the remains of a workman's lunch and drank some water from a puddle. As the night grew colder, he trotted back to his carton home and fell asleep in the middle of a mew.

He shivered in his sleep. There were no warm bodies to snuggle under, no comforting chirps from his mother, no sound of other breathing, other heartbeats. Just his own.

2

Growing Up

Early next morning, Mosby went to the place where he had last seen his family. He walked on the scaffold and sniffed at the board slanting downward into the darkness far below. He listened. There was no sound, no sign of his family. He waited, mewing forlornly. Where were they? Why didn't they come back?

They didn't come back because they couldn't get back. The very morning they left, cement trucks had poured the last foundations. All the cats were outside the building eating Ed's free meal, all but Mosby. Now he was trapped inside, behind the steep foundation walls.

After a few days, he stopped looking for his family. He was lonely, but he had a bigger problem. Food. Luckily, the workmen usually left some in the trash. Aside from these scraps, which were not exactly a banquet, there was a tantalizing amount of live game around, even in the open structure of cement and steel. There were insects—flies, moths and butterflies, even crickets. There were rats and mice and birds of all kinds—sparrows and starlings and pigeons. Dozens of pigeons! They seemed so fat and lazy they looked easy to catch. Mosby sneaked up on one, moving each paw ever so slowly. But when he pounced, his claws clutched only a feather or two, nothing more. It was puzzling, this flying business.

Mosby pounced on a fly hovering over a pile of trash. The angry buzzing tickled his paws. When he peeked in to have a closer look at his prize, the thing whizzed away. With practice, he became an expert fly catcher. But it took a lot of flies to make a meal. And they weren't all that tasty anyway, mostly wings and buzz.

So he concentrated on the food the workmen brought. Stealing a sandwich was dangerous work. Once a hairy hand caught him and snatched him up, squeezing the breath out of him. In terror, Mosby scratched and bit. There was a yell and the fingers let him go. Mosby ran. The man hurled a stone after him. It hit Mosby on the leg and sent him spinning. He crawled into a dark corner and licked and licked the sore place, his eyes dark with hurt and fear. He never forgot that day. He was learning: DON'T TRUST PEOPLE.

The Kennedy Center was growing. So was the small gray cat. Mosby survived—lean, fast, clever and brave—wild as wild and trusting no one. He knew his territory, every beam, every vent, every hole a cat could slip into. He knew how to move without being seen. By night he prowled all over his building, by day he vanished into the dark, secret places, only coming out to hunt or steal a meal. As the building grew, he moved upward and inward, retreating from the people.

By and by, the Kennedy Center was finished on the outside. From the acres of parking lots underground to the flat roof, the marble walls rose, gleaming whitely beside the river. The shiny-hats left. New people came. New sounds echoed everywhere—carpenters, plasterers, plumbers, electricians. They built inside walls, hung doors, plastered ceilings. They lined the great long hall with mirrors that caught the afternoon sun. They covered the floor of the hall from end to end with a warm red carpet so soft that even the heavy footsteps of people made no sound. The place blossomed with lights hung from the ceilings high overhead.

There was one area on the top floor they left unfinished. It was a strange place of many levels and dark corners. On one side, high up, was a window wall looking out on the river. No one came there. This became Mosby's special place, his Hideout, safe from the people, their bustle and their noise.

From here, he wandered around his territory, watching everything happening in the building. After the fire doors were set in place, it was hard to get off the top floor. But the top floor was a vast area, with plenty to see.

One day, he found a passage below the floor of his Hideout that led to a small platform, a special place, almost a nest, in the false ceiling over one of the theaters. He watched workmen hanging a huge red and black curtain. They brought in hundreds of seats and set them all facing the curtain. Mosby couldn't imagine what they were for.

But he was learning about seats. A new breed of people had moved into a long row of offices right outside his Hideout. They worked for the American Film Institute, or A.F.I, an organization dedicated to the art of movies and TV. These people didn't curl up in a corner like any respectable cat, or straddle a beam like a shiny-hat. They sat on chairs. They had desks and typewriters and telephones. In fact Mosby's world had a whole new sound—the hum of elevators, the small tap-tap of the typewriters and the ear-tickling ring of the phones.

One day, he found a way into the ceiling of another theater. In the semi-darkness, he watched workmen hanging a shining glass design, talking and laughing as they worked.

"Now try it!" someone shouted. Suddenly, the ceiling blazed with a spangle of lights like the stars outside his night window, only closer and somehow brighter. Mosby looked and looked. There was a silence in the theater. The workmen were all gazing up at the lights, too. Finally, someone said softly, "O.K. That'll do." The lights went out. Mosby trotted back to his Hideout with the stars still shining in his eyes.

He would really have enjoyed life if he just hadn't been so hungry. Now that the building was closed in and civilized, it was getting harder and harder to find enough to eat. He had practically eliminated the mouse and rat population, and he could no longer get at the birds. These new people hardly ever left scraps around. He was becoming desperate.

*   *   *

Asleep in his Hideout after an unsuccessful night of hunting, Mosby dreamed he was chasing a mouse; his paws twitched. Just then, a tangy odor curled out of the air vent over his head and tickled his nose. His dream-mouse turned into . . . HAMBURGER! Suddenly Mosby was wide awake.

HAMBURGER? Up to now, he had tasted only cold, gray bits of hamburger left in the trash. But he knew this was just the thing for a hungry cat. His mouth began to water. He leapt up into the vent where the faint but enticing smell led him to passages he had not travelled in some time.

Ahead of him, a door was open a crack. He forgot caution. He forgot the first rule of cats: stop, look, listen. Never pass through a doorway without first checking for danger.

Mosby didn't notice the man in the white hat at the stove, the waitresses bustling about. He darted out into the kitchen and leapt up onto a hot tray of hamburgers. For a moment, the whole kitchen stopped moving. Everyone froze, mouths open and eyes staring. Then everything started to happen at once, like a speeded-up movie.

The hot tray burned Mosby's feet. He howled and sprang into the air.

The man in the white hat yelled, "Get it! Catch it!" Someone threw something. Mosby dodged and slipped through a swinging door. He was in a roomful of people sitting at tables, eating. The man in the white hat was right behind him. Mosby ran for all of his nine lives. He scuttled between feet, under the chairs and tables, trying to find a hiding place. A hand clutched at him. He leapt up onto a table. In midair, the startled cat confronted a startled face. Mosby made a valiant effort to change direction. It was too late. Most of him landed in a bowl of soup.

In one sloppy bound he reached the top of a booth, slithering along, leaving a splatter of greasy pawprints. At the end of the booth, he slipped to the floor and sped back through the swinging door. In the wink of an eye, he was gone. Only one person saw him go.

A shy secretary named Jan, who was lunching alone in a corner booth, saw the whole thing: the frantic chase, the cat's terror. She felt that terror herself. She sat very still, her heart pounding.

"Where did it go?" shouted the man in the white hat.

"What WAS it?" asked a waitress.

The shy secretary found herself whispering, "I hope he got away! I hope he got away!"

Gradually things calmed down. The man in the white hat went back to his cooking. The cafeteria manager and the

"In mid-air, he made a valiant effort to change direction."

waitresses wiped up the soup and reassured the startled customers. Safe inside his vent, Mosby paused. The scent of hamburger was still strong. Before retreating to the safety of his Hideout, he crouched down and howled, his ears flat against his head.

The secretary heard him. Her eyes sparkled. He did get away! A young man who had just come into the restaurant, paused by the booth where she was sitting.

"Now, what in the world was that?" he asked nobody in particular. The secretary smiled shyly up at the man and stammered, "It—it sounded like a . . . well . . . you know . . . like a cat."

"A WHAT?" The young man grinned at her.

"I've got to admit it sure sounded like a cat," he said. "But . . ."

That was what most of the people thought. There were few who had actually seen Mosby—the waitress and the man in the white hat—and the soup-eater. Someone who has had a live cat spring out of nowhere into his bowl of soup doesn't forget it. But the rest, frankly, were not so sure what they had seen. And like rational people who think they've seen a flying saucer, they were not too anxious to talk about it.

Later on, people in the kitchen joked about the day the ghost-cat got loose in the cafeteria. The news finally reached Ed.

"It's possible," he said in a distracted way. "This building is full of surprises. But how could a cat climb up five stories to our new cafeteria? Firedoors shut off the stairs. Cats don't usually take elevators. So how—?"

No one knew the answer. It was a mystery. Hardly anyone took seriously the idea that a cat might actually be living in the Kennedy Center. Not yet.

The shy secretary had her suspicions, but she kept them to herself.

Mosby never went back to the cafeteria again. There was food there, but he wasn't welcome. They had made that plain. After the terror of that day's chase, he was much more careful to stay out of sight. He hunted only at night, after everyone had left his building. He found very little to eat, and he grew thinner and weaker every day.

3

Discovered

Jan was humming a little song to herself as the fire door slammed behind her. It was her lunch hour and she had wandered into the unfinished theater looking for a little peace and quiet. Jan was a secretary, which means she did a lot of typing and made coffee and answered the phone and said "Yes, Sir!" a lot to her boss, who was the Head Builder. Things were always in a crisis and her life was rather hectic.

Jan groped her way across the floor. It was sort of spooky in here. High overhead, maybe three stories up, some bare bulbs glimmered, leaving the vast place dark and mysterious. She shivered. Up on one side behind a sort of platform, she could see daylight. There must be windows there, she thought.

A semicircle of cement steps, like an ancient Greek amphitheater, led upward. In the dim light, she moved carefully toward them, then stopped with a gasp. One step ahead was a drop off to the bottom floor of the theater 30 feet below. She could barely see it in the dim grayness. Instinctively, she backed away from the edge and tiptoed up the steps toward the light.

At the top of the steps, a ladder left behind by the workmen led up to a high platform, maybe the place for the spotlights when the theater was finished. She climbed up, thinking what an adventure this was. Soon she stood on the platform in the welcome light, facing a wall of large, dusty windows shimmering with sunlight. Jan paused, spreading out her arms. The view was unbelievable. For a moment, she just looked. Then, ever so quietly so as not to disturb the silence, she sat down, dangling her legs over the edge.

Beyond the white roof-terrace, the river spread out beneath her, sparkling in the sun. A jet hung noiseless above the Virginia shore. A sightseeing boat moved slowly around a bend in the river, vanishing under a bridge. No noise came through the soundproof glass; it was like a silent movie. Away over the trees, she could see the spires and smokestacks of Georgetown and the distant Cathedral. Close by, a corner of the new Watergate building jutted into view.

Jan listened. Way down, behind the fire door, where the offices of the American Film Institute were, she heard laughter and a phone ringing. She felt like Alice in Wonderland. She had slipped through the looking glass into another world. She liked this place; she tried to think why. No red carpets, chandeliers or marble here. Just the bare bones of the building, gray cement blocks and red steel girders stretching upward like the beams of a giant, empty barn. She felt she had found the heart of the building.

Jan unwrapped her tuna sandwich. Then, suddenly, she sat very still. Something or someone was there. She heard a faint rustle, like a snake slipping through dry leaves. The hair on the back of her neck prickled. She could hear her heart beating very fast. She held her breath, listening.

"Behind a platform she could see daylight."

Out of the corner of her eye, she saw something. It was a small, grayish shadow within a shadow. She turned her head very slowly. Dazzled by the sunshine, she tried to see into the darkness beyond a cement wall that jutted out onto the ledge. Something moved. She gasped. Then the thing vanished.

It was a cat!

She was sure of it, a skinny cat, all fur and ribs and eyes! She remembered the cat in the cafeteria. "It must be the same one," she thought. "So this is where he hides, in this deserted place! Poor thing, he's starving."

"Kitty, kitty?" she whispered. "Come on out; I won't hurt you." She held out her hand and saw it was shaking.

"Really, Jan, scared by a little cat!" She took a deep breath. "Whew! But you did scare me, Puss! . . . Here!" She held out a piece of her sandwich toward the shadowy place where she had seen the cat.

"Come on," she coaxed. "Have a bite to eat; you must be very hungry." She tossed the bit of bread toward the shadows.

There was no sound, no sign of the cat.

Now Mosby—for of course, it was Mosby—WAS starving. He hadn't eaten in so long he was weak and dizzy. But somehow, he could not come out in the open. He was wild and trusted no one. Jan coaxed and called, but it was no use.

"Oh, well, maybe I just imagined it," she said. But in her heart she knew better. She had seen a cat. It was like when you look into a bright light, then close your eyes, an image of that light shines behind your eyelids. So Jan, after only a flash, could still see the ghostly cat.

She started to eat her sandwich, but she couldn't seem to swallow. She felt eyes watching her—hungry eyes.

"Oh, all right. You can have it. I don't seem to be very hungry."

She broke her sandwich into pieces and laid them carefully

on her paper napkin. Then she got up slowly and brushed off her skirt.

"I have to get back to work."

She started down the ladder and then paused, listening.

"Puss?" she said softly. "Kitty, kitty?"

There was no sound. She sighed and climbed down into the shadows. Pausing by the door at the bottom, she called, "I'll bring you some milk before I go home. I'll be back; I promise."

Her voice sounded small and far away. The young man from the cafeteria stood in the doorway.

"Oh, there you are, Jan. Your boss is after you. Who were you talking to?"

"No one . . . that is . . . I thought I saw something."

"What did you see?" He peered at her. "You're so pale, you look like you saw a ghost."

"Well, sort of a ghost. I saw . . . I saw a . . . a cat."

"A what? A cat? Here, in the Kennedy Center? Come on, you must be kidding!"

"I'm not. I'm serious. I saw it, just for a second, a gray, starving cat."

"Sure, Jan, sure you saw a cat. Probably the same one you saw in the cafeteria." His teasing made her angry. But before she could answer him, he said, "Come on, your boss wants you."

"You don't believe me, but I saw him, like a gray ghost . . ."

The door slammed. Mosby listened. No sound. They had gone. He waited to be sure. Then carefully, he sneaked over to the food. Carefully, he sniffed it. The pure, sweet smell of tuna! His mouth watered! He simply DEVOURED the sandwich. Then he licked every crumb off the napkin. When he was sure there was no more, he drank from a nearby puddle of water. (He never went thirsty, as there were several leaks in the roof.)

Then he washed his thin, scraggly fur and lay down in a patch of sun. A warmth spread through his body, and from deep down inside, there came just the faintest, rusty rumble. He was purring. It had been such a long time since he had purred!

Jan did come back late that afternoon. Mosby heard the door slam and slipped into the shadows. She climbed up to the ledge where the western sun slanted through the window-wall. The ledge was empty. The sandwich was gone.

"I knew it! I was not imagining. You're in here somewhere, aren't you, Cat?"

She peered into the shadows. After looking around guiltily as if someone might be watching, she set down a plastic container of cottage cheese and milk.

"There you are, little gray ghost."

Then a thought lit up her face.

"Gray ghost! That's it! I'll call you Mosby, after that Civil War colonel, John Mosby. He was nicknamed 'The Gray Ghost' because he would slip in and out of enemy lines unseen. He knew the hills and trails of the Shenandoah Valley the same way you know the vents and air ducts and hidden places of this building! Mosby, the Gray Ghost. That name suits you, too."

"Mosby?" she said softly. "Mosby." It sounded just right. "How do you like that name?" She listened as if expecting an answer, then made her way down to the door. "I'll bring you some more tomorrow, Mosby."

And she did.

And that's how Mosby got his name. I've called him Mosby from the beginning, but to tell the truth, this is the first time anyone had called him anything except DUMB CAT!

24

4

Jan

After Jan discovered Mosby, life brightened for both of them. He no longer had to worry about food all the time; she was needed. It made them both feel warm and good. Every lunch hour, she climbed up to the ledge with fresh food and milk for Mosby. She brought up a folding chair, used an empty crate for a table and settled herself by the window to eat her own lunch.

She never tired of the view, always changing, always the same: the jets in the sky, the boats on the river, the cars endlessly crossing the bridges. Sitting there behind the glass wall, she felt apart from all that life rushing somewhere, anywhere. She thought she had discovered a secret, but she wasn't quite sure what it was.

At first, Mosby didn't think too much of this invasion of his Hideout. He crouched in the shadows, his tail twitching impatiently. He wished the intruder would go away so he could eat.

But cats like routine, so along about noon, he found himself listening for the fire door's slam and the light footsteps climbing up to the ledge. He liked these regular meals, something he hadn't had since he was a kitten.

As time went by, Mosby began to notice Jan, not just the food she brought, but her voice, her step, her smell. Gradually, his fear lessened. Then, even more gradually, he became aware of a strange and unfamiliar feeling. When he heard her step, a sort of warmth, like purring, like sunshine, spread through him.

Jan, too, looked forward to these quiet noontimes. She started talking to her invisible cat, telling him her troubles.

"It's hard living alone in a strange city," Jan said one noon, sitting in her usual spot and staring out the window. "Life is so hectic." She sighed. "There are so many things you can't possibly know about, Mosby. Things like traffic and getting your feet wet and being scared to walk alone at night."

She nibbled at her sandwich. Mosby's mouth watered as he watched her from his hiding place behind a beam.

"Eating alone! That's no fun, either. Somehow nothing tastes any good. Maybe it's the silence. Sometimes I turn on some dumb TV show, just so there's noise in my apartment."

Jan paused and listened.

"How come the silence at home is so depressing, and here, it's peaceful?"

Mosby was beginning to think Jan would never go when she rose finally and whispered, "Well, have a good lunch— bye." She climbed down the ladder, whistling softly to herself. As soon as she was out of sight, he crept out and started eating.

Just outside the fire door, Jan almost bumped into the young man. He always seemed to be hanging around the drinking fountain.

"Have you seen it?" he asked, smiling.

"Seen what?" Jan asked, her thoughts still back in the unfinished theater behind the fire door.

"Did you see the thing again?"

"Mosby's a cat, not a thing. No, I haven't seen him—not yet. But he's there. His dish is always empty."

"Maybe you're just feeding the local rat." The young man laughed. Jan felt her cheeks grow hot. She turned and walked away fast. She hated that young man, him and his laugh!

One noon, the fire door slammed as usual, but the footsteps climbing up sounded most unusual. It was Jan, all right, but her step was heavy. She plunked Mosby's dish down so hard the milk spilled.

"Oh, boy, Mosby, thank God you're not a secretary!" She sat down so heavily the chair creaked. Mosby's ears flattened. "Things are always going wrong, and then my Boss gets mad at me."

Her voice had started out angry, but it suddenly got higher and weaker and dissolved in little snufflings and sobbings. People were a puzzle. Mosby's ears pricked. Finally, the snuffling stopped. There was a sort of explosion into her handkerchief. Mosby jumped.

Jan blew her nose again. "When my boss gets mad," she said, "I make mistakes. I couldn't spell today, I couldn't even type! Something's up. My Boss never used to act this way—touchy and cross . . ."

Jan sighed a big sigh. "Mosby? Are you really there? Are you listening? I keep telling you my troubles—and here you are, probably the most alone creature in the whole world. All, all alone, surrounded by this, this . . ."

She looked behind her at the cement steps facing the darkened theater—steps that one day would hold seats for the audience—waiting, always waiting, for the play to begin. She sighed and turned back toward the window.

Outside, a family strolled on the balcony. Tourists. They peered in the window, shielding their eyes, trying to see beyond their own reflections and the dazzle of the white marble terrace.

They couldn't see the solitary figure watching them from her perch on the folding chair. There was an invisible wall separating them, more than the window. Jan was a watcher, caught in a web of silence on the inside of the glass. They, the tourists, were the unwitting actors—and Life was the play.

They would never know, could never guess, what was there beyond the glass.

In pantomime, they took pictures of the view and of each other, held hands, pulled their children away from the edge and moved on. Jan suddenly felt very alone.

"I wonder if Mosby is lonely," she thought. "If you have never had a friend, can you call that empty feeling loneliness?"

Jan was motionless, lost in thought. Suddenly, she was aware of something moving behind her on the ledge. She froze. She hardly dared breath. Slowly, a lean, gray cat melted out of the shadow. He crept in slow motion toward the bowl of food. It was Mosby! The cat stalked the dish, ears back, his body low, moving so slowly that she could hardly see him change position. Although his eyes were held by the food, she knew he was aware of her.

It seemed forever before he reached the dish. Then, in a few gulps, the food was gone.

"He's like a wild animal," she thought, "ready to run at any moment." She hardly dared breathe. He began lapping the milk. He glanced up at her every few seconds. "He IS a wild animal," she realized. Jan studied Mosby carefully. He was still very thin, but not the skeleton-cat she had seen a month ago. "Well, he ought to look better," she thought, "after all the food I've brought him."

He was gray, the color of smoke, the gray of shadows. His whiskers were long and black; his tongue was bright pink as it flashed in and out. She noticed he had a faint M mark on his forehead and a slight nick in his right ear. His eyes—his eyes seemed to glow. Were they gold? Were they green? She

"Suddenly she was aware of something moving behind her on the
ledge."

couldn't tell. "How uncomfortable you are when you try to sit completely still!" she thought. Her foot was going to sleep. Her nose tickled. She tried not to think about the tickle, but it suddenly exploded in a sneeze. Like a puff of smoke, Mosby was gone.

"Darn!" she muttered, as she stretched her cramped legs. Then a slow smile lighted her face.

Not everybody would understand her happiness. But those watchers who wait patiently for a glimpse of the shy, wild creatures of this world—a glimpse into that wildness from which we all come—THEY will understand.

A hymn from her childhood came into her head.

"Ye watchers and ye holy ones . . ."

Jan hummed it softly to herself as she climbed down the steps. As she passed the drinking fountain, the young man was standing there, as usual. Before he could tease her, she straightened her shoulders and smiled up at him, smugly.

"I saw him," she said. "Mosby. He's a big, gray cat, and he's getting fat." She sailed off down the hall, leaving the young man staring.

*   *   *

Jan didn't see Mosby again for more than a week. A sneeze is a startling sound. But after he recovered from the shock, he began creeping out every day while Jan was having her lunch.

His manner improved with his confidence. His slink became a stride; he held his tail high; his eyes began to look more curious than scared. But he was still cautious. If Jan moved suddenly, be fled.

"No one is going to catch or take you anywhere, Mosby. I can see that." Jan could see more. She was looking at a miracle, a miracle she herself had created. Steady food and love had changed a scrawny, cringing creature into a proud, fat cat.

Mosby's coat shone in the sun. She yearned to touch it, let him feel a loving hand. Maybe someday, if she was patient, he might let her take him home. Mosby, who had been grooming himself at the other end of the ledge, rose and glanced at Jan as if he had read her mind. He stalked off, swishing his tail, bent around a corner and disappeared out of sight.

It was a dramatic exit.

"How he has changed!" Jan thought.

She didn't notice, but she was changing, too. Her love for the cat had filled her deep loneliness. Now, suddenly it was spring. The city seemed warm and friendly. She had started exploring with the young man, who had stopped being a tease and started being a friend—a good friend! They joined the strollers wandering beneath the cherry blossoms. The air was soft. Birds sang. Jan caught herself laughing for no reason at all. She started looking forward to her weekends. The city was so full of wonderful things to do.

5

The Parties

Now that Mosby was well fed, he could relax and enjoy his building. Something was always happening. As Mosby wandered here and there, investigating every new development, sightings of a ghostly cat were reported to Ed, the building manager, in his downstairs office. There, like the captain of a great ship, he supervised the running of the building. Ed thought it "possible, but very unlikely" that a cat would be living somewhere in the Kennedy Center. He was very busy. The plays and concerts were scheduled to begin soon. These rumors of a ghost-cat seemed unimportant compared to all of his other problems.

But to Henri, the banquet manager, the ghost-cat was more than a rumor. Something—some thief—was after his beautifully laid out tables. And that something certainly had a good appetite—for a ghost. You see, countries all over the world started giving things to the Kennedy Center. All the white marble came from Italy. The Japanese made a vast, red-and-gold silk curtain for the Opera House. Sweden and Ireland gave the glittering chandeliers; Belgium, huge mirrors. Those kinds of things. So a committee formed to plan luncheons and banquets, to thank everyone for the gifts and to encourage more.

One afternoon, Mosby awoke from a snooze with barely a yawn. Strange noises told him something was going on. He sped down the steps and into a vent to the North Gallery to investigate. Peering around a corner, he saw tables set up against a far wall—tables covered with crisp white cloths.

There was a clinking of glasses and a clattering of dishes as waiters carried in large trays. The sounds reminded Mosby of something unpleasant—that awful day in the cafeteria. He turned, about to flee, when a new smell made him pause. What was it? He sniffed again and made up his mind. Whatever it was smelled so delicious he just had to have a taste. He couldn't help himself.

Mosby watched for his chance. When there was a pause in the rushing back and forth of black trousers, a gray shadow whisked unnoticed across the floor and under a white tablecloth. The waiters brought in the last of the food and left. All was still—all but the soft hiss of the burners keeping things warm and the delicate aromas teasing one very sensitive cat nose. Mosby waited. When no one came, he eased out from under the cloth.

A cat's leap is a marvel—not like a bird's, with flutterings—more like a fish's, a gesture of fluid grace. One moment Mosby was crouching below, then there was a blur of fur and he landed lightly among the platters.

Before him stretched a feast fit for the most discriminating cat—steaming platters of chicken, lobster Newburg and rice—a circle of pink shrimp nestled in a bed of chipped ice beside a dish of caviar. There were boards of assorted cheeses and plates of little dainties, deviled eggs, tiny half-sandwiches of rolled

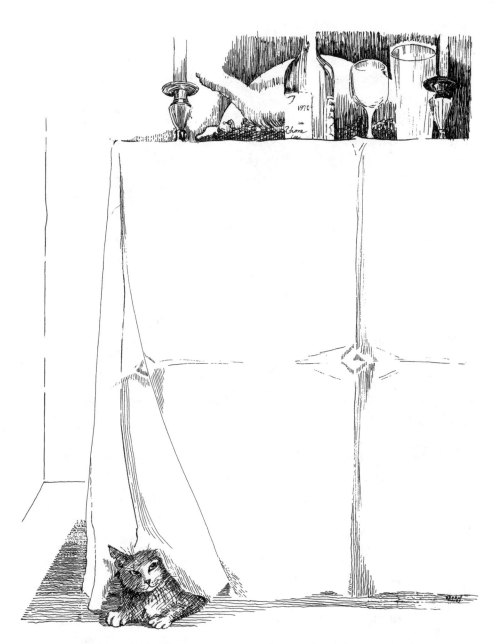

"Mosby waited. When no one came, he eased out from under the cloth."

anchovies and thin slices of rare beef. In his haste to sample everything, Mosby wasn't exactly neat. In fact, he left a trail of chewed bits and crumbs as he wound delicately between the wineglasses and candlesticks.

Footsteps and a slamming door sent Mosby flying for his vent, a shrimp tight in his teeth. While he finished his meal and wash-up safe in his Hideout, Henri was raging and the waiters were hurriedly cleaning up the tables before the guests arrived. Someone or something had been at his banquet, and Henri, in unintelligible French, was calling on his Gallic Gods to help him find and punish the thief.

The "thief" was delighted with this new source of supplies. Quite a change from the shiny-hats sandwiches of long ago, far tastier than Jan's cat food and cottage cheese. Mosby's ears became sensitive to the sounds of a party setting up. At the first faint clink of glasses, he would trot down and wait for his chance to sample Henri's menu. The banquet manager became more and more frustrated. Whenever the tables were left unguarded, there was evidence a local gourmet had checked things out.

One night, before the guests arrived, Henri tiptoed into the North Gallery and surprised one large, gray cat making off with a chicken breast in hollandaise. Henri's assistant, hearing some rather rude French sounds, found his boss rushing around the banquet table, shouting "Shoo!" and other things to an empty room. Word spread among the waiters that the pressure of all these parties had finally gotten to their boss.

Now that he knew what "It" was, Henri secretly set a variety of traps. Henri was a chef and not a trapper, so his traps were pretty primitive: a big rat trap, set with cheese for bait, easy for a fast-moving cat to "out paw"; other devices made of pots and dish covers, food boxes and string. Nothing worked. The bait was stolen, the thief was untrappable.

After Mosby discovered the traps, he grew more cautious than ever. He still attended the parties, but carefully out of sight. After sampling the fare, he often stayed watching from under cover. The sounds of a party are the same the world over—laughter, chatter, glasses clinking. It's a nice sound, peculiar to Man, the social animal. Mosby liked it.

These people were not like any he'd encountered before. They sounded different. They smelled different. They acted different. They drank a lot, but it was bitter stuff. He tried some once—just once. It wasn't soda or milk, that's for sure. But their food—that was delicious. No wonder his coat grew shinier!

For a while now, Mosby had felt something in the air—something contagious—an electricity, as if some Big Thing was about to happen. He didn't know what. Then, suddenly, one night, the theaters opened, and the plays and music began.

6

Mosby Makes the Papers

The first night of any performance is called an "opening." For the Kennedy Center, this was a double opening. Both the theaters and the building itself were having their "first night." The place had been humming for days, but this was different. The murmur of many voices is an awesome sound. Mosby crawled down to his special place in the false ceiling to see what was up. He tucked his paws under his chest and watched. Far below him, looking very small, people sat in those rows of seats, all facing the same direction.

Mosby had wondered for some time what this place was for. More and more people came until the floor below was aflutter with humanity. Mosby's heart pounded. He had never seen so many people before in his life. They made a strange noise, like buzzing, like flies. A bell sounded far off. The lights overhead dimmed, and the buzzing suddenly stopped, as if turned off by the light switch. In the darkness there were little flutterings and sparkles and coughings, as if the people were all settling down for the night. Mosby yawned. Then he stopped with his mouth still opened wide. The curtain-wall parted silently. Behind it was a room bright with sunshine, although Mosby had watched the sun set not too long before.

People came in and out, wandering about this room. They looked like the people he watched on the terrace, only now he could hear them. They laughed and cried and talked—oh how they talked!—until Mosby, like many a theatergoer before him, found his eyes growing heavy. He dozed.

He was awakened by a noise that sent him scurrying back to the safety of his Hideout. After many nights spent watching what went on in the brightly lit place beyond the curtain, he finally figured out the cause of the roaring sound. It was the people in the seats slapping their hands together, a strange custom he never quite got used to. Sometimes there was another noise that made his skin twitch. He had heard the shiny-hats and Jan's young man make the sound, but it was different when hundreds of people did it all together. Every so often, with no warning, great waves of laughter pounded his sensitive ears.

One night, it was too much. Mosby answered this racket with a YOWL! Now, most of the people sitting in the theater that night must have heard Mosby's yell. If they had been awakened by such a sound outside the bedroom, they would have recognized it. But a catcall in a theater? Nonsense! There was one person who heard and really listened. It was a newspaper reporter. She nudged her companion and whispered, "Did you hear that?"

The companion, intent on the play, paid no attention.

"Didn't you hear it?" she persisted. "That was a tomcat, no mistake!"

The people sitting around her glared. Her companion shushed her.

"I know I heard a cat," she continued.

There was a chorus of shushes all around her. The newspaperwoman sank down in her seat and muttered under her breath. She forgot the play—she was listening hard for another catcall. But Mosby had gone off to watch the night sky from his window.

The next day, the newspaperwoman came back to the Kennedy Center and started asking the question: "Is it possible there is a cat living here?" The souvenir sellers gave her strange looks. A guard moved away without looking her in the eyes. Some guides smiled and shook their heads. She began to think she had imagined the whole thing, as her companion last night had assured her. But while she was up in the cafeteria having lunch, a waitress remembered.

"A cat in the Kennedy Center? No! How could there be . . . but wait. There was one time . . . a wild cat or something got loose in the kitchens . . ."

The reporter's eyes widened. "Aha! A wild cat? Did you see it?"

"Well, no, not exactly. That was before I came . . . it landed in a bowl of soup . . . made an awful mess, they say."

"Do you know anyone who actually saw this . . . this cat?"

The waitress shrugged. "No. They used to joke about it around here, that's all."

"Did they say what happened to it?" The reporter felt she was getting close.

"It just . . . just vanished." The waitress shook her head. "That's what they say . . . it vanished . . ."

"What do you mean, 'vanished'? That cat must have gone somewhere—"

Jan's young man happened to be in the next booth and over-

41

heard the questions about the cat. He peered around the booth and grinned at the reporter.

"Lady," he said, "if you come with me, I think I know someone who can shed some light on the mystery of the vanishing cat."

He brought her to see Jan. And that's how Mosby got in the newspapers.

*   *   *

As the fire door opened at its usual time a few days later, Mosby's ears twitched. Along with Jan's usual gentle footsteps, there were other steps, noisier, firmer. Mosby hid in the shadows as Jan and a strange woman climbed up to the window ledge. Jan set down his food in the usual place, then joined the stranger at the far end of the ledge. Mosby watched, ears back, his heart beating fast. There was no sound. Mosby studied the stranger holding a black box in her lap. Mosby waited, every sense alert. Jan spoke, her voice smoothing the tenseness in the air.

"It's all right, Mosby . . . Puss? Come on; have your lunch. It's all right. It's only me. I just brought a friend."

Mosby felt his muscles relax at the sound of the familiar voice. But he was still suspicious. He also was very hungry. It had been a long weekend, with no parties. He watched the stranger, who sat so still holding that black box. He felt no vibes of danger. He waited. They waited. Finally, slowly, ever so slowly, he moved out of the shadows toward the plate of food. His eyes darted back and forth between the stranger and the bowl. When he was almost there, he stopped and looked up for an instant frozen forever in time . . .

CLICK! Something exploded in the little black box. For an instant, Mosby was blinded. He stood there, dazed, his eyes dizzy with orange suns. Then he vanished.

42

But not before the box had caught Mosby—not his real self, but his image. It was proof for all the world that there was a real cat in the Kennedy Center.

The stranger had taken his picture!

7

Jan Says Goodbye

After the story of Mosby appeared in the newspapers, the cat was out of the bag. Messages and letters came in to the Center full of advice on how to catch a cat. Jan wished she had never told anyone about Mosby, but it was too late now. There were others who wished she had kept quiet. Roger was really upset. As the Chairman, his dream—a center of culture in the nation's capital—finally had come true. And now, here was this story of a wild cat bumming around in his building! A Center for stray cats! Good grief!

Ed had an uneasy feeling. He remembered all those other rumors about a cat in the building. He called Jan down to his office to ask her about the story in the paper. At first she was scared, but as she told Ed about finding and feeding the cat, she began to relax. When she got to the part where Mosby finally appeared to her, they both were smiling.

"He ate lunch with me every day until the picture. The

flash must have scared him. I haven't seen him since." Jan sighed.

"That's some story, young lady," said Ed.

Jan was surprised. "You believe me?"

"Of course I do. Why would you lie about a thing like that?"

Jan liked this man. "Sir, there's one thing that has always puzzled me: how do you suppose he got inside in the first place?"

Ed was silent, remembering all those cats in his headlights so long ago. "Probably he was born here and grew up inside the building. There were lots of cats hanging around when we started construction . . . 50 or more. I used to feed them all . . ."

"So you're a cat nut, too!" said Jan.

"A what?"

"A lover of stray cats."

"I fed the cats to keep them around. We had a rat problem," said Ed brusquely. Jan nodded, grinning, as if she knew a secret.

"You're still feeding this cat," Ed asked, all business, "up in that godforsaken place?"

"Yup. Every day."

"We've just got to get him out of there," Ed muttered.

"How?" Jan interrupted. "You can't catch him; he's too wild."

Ed scratched his head. "That empty theater is a huge place."

"You'll never find him in there," Jan added.

"It's a tough problem," Ed agreed.

"Oh, wait. Here's something." Jan took an envelope out of a folder. "I got a letter today. This might help. Advice from someone who caught a wild cat abandoned at a summer campground. Their tame Siamese lured this wild cat out. They say all we have to do is bring a tame cat into . . ."

"We've enough trouble with one cat," Ed interrupted, taking the letter hastily. "Did you bring me the, um, the data . . . on this cat?"

"Here." Jan handed Ed the folder. "Here are all the facts you asked for . . . all the letters and phone calls . . . his diet . . ."

Ed rocked his chair back, tapped the folder against his hand and gazed at something far off beyond the ceiling.

"You're still feeding him?" he asked dreamily.

"Oh, yes, but I haven't seen him . . . lately."

"But he's still there?" Ed stopped rocking and leaned forward, looking Jan in the eyes. "You are sure he's still there?"

Jan was startled by his sudden, sharp question.

"Of course I'm sure." She looked right back at him, her jaw firm. "He's there, all right." Ed nodded and leaned back in his chair again.

"We've got to get him out of there," he whispered.

"Yes," Jan agreed, "before the workmen go in there to finish the place. They would really scare him."

"Yeah," Ed nodded. "They'd scare him for sure, but . . ." Ed cleared his throat, paused, as if thinking over his next remark, then leaned forward and said in a low voice, "Now, I wouldn't want this repeated around . . ." he waited.

"I won't say a word," whispered Jan.

"Well, we're not going to finish that theater . . . at least, not right now . . ."

"You're not going to finish the theater?" Jan's voice bubbled with relief.

"Not right now," Ed answered heavily. "We've got problems . . . building costs are . . . out of sight."

"Well, then. Everything's O.K. I mean, Mosby will be safe!"

Ed sighed and looked at Jan a long moment. "That's one way of looking at it, young lady. The cat will be safe."

"You don't understand. I've been so worried," Jan went on. "You see . . . I've got a problem . . ."

"I understand, but just keep feeding him," Ed interrupted. "Now, if that's all about the cat . . ." His secretary appeared in the doorway. "Here," he waved the folder at her. "Start a new file, M for Mosby." The secretary looked puzzled. "Our resident cat," Ed explained. Then he turned to Jan and said, "Send down anything new on him, so we'll know where we stand."

"Here are the estimates you asked for." The secretary set down a pile of papers. Ed picked up a pencil and started ruffling through the pile. With a sigh, Jan rose. At the door she paused and took a deep breath. She held her hands together to stop her fingers from trembling. She cleared her throat. Ed looked up and saw Jan still standing there.

"Well?"

"I . . . I'm going to be leaving soon."

"Oh? Sorry to hear that." Ed was studying the papers again.

"I . . . I'm going to get married." There, it was out. Jan's cheeks grew pink.

"Unhuh." It was the sound people make when they're not listening.

Jan waited. Her cheeks grew pinker. "I, that is, we, are moving back to Philadelphia."

She had said it. Her heart was pounding. The man bending over his desk looked up suddenly.

"What? What did you say?"

"I'm going away," she said loudly. "When I go, who's going to feed Mosby?"

"Get someone else." Ed sounded impatient. "There must be lots of . . . um . . . cat nuts up there in those A.F.I. offices. Get one of them. If the cat is as wild as you say, it won't matter to him who feeds him, just as long as he's fed.

The phone rang. Ed waved at Jan. "Let me know who you get." He picked up the phone.

"Hello?" It was Roger. Ed listened a moment, then said, "Yes, sir. You mean that cat story in the paper?" He picked up a pencil and started doodling a picture of a cat. "Yes, sir, I believe it's true . . . Yes, sir . . . I mean no, sir, I know we can't have that kind of thing . . ." The doodle started to look like a dragon. "Bad for our image, yes. I understand . . . He won't be easy to catch, but I'm working on it . . . Well, it's a big place for a cat to hide . . ." The dragon had smoke coming out of his nostrils. Ed covered the phone with his hand and whispered to Jan, still standing at the door, "Just keep me posted."

Jan tiptoed out. She took Mosby's food from her desk and went up to the Hideout. She had to think. Mosby was nowhere around. She set the dish down, then settled herself on her chair. She had felt guilty about leaving, but Mosby would be safe now, if his Hideout were left undisturbed. She looked around at this place where she had spend so many happy hours. Maybe Ed was right. Mosby didn't really need her . . . all he needed was a good, daily meal. She frowned. "I guess I needed you more than you needed me, cat." She started sadly down the steps. The fire door opened below. It was the young man.

"Jan?" he held out his hand. "Come on! I'm taking you to lunch, remember?" She laughed and hurried toward him.

"I'm coming!" she called.

In the following days, Jan did everything to make sure Mosby would be all right. She easily found people to feed him when she left. There were several cat lovers in the offices right outside his Hideout. Her job kept her so busy, she started leaving Mosby's food in a dark corner just inside the fire door, first thing in the morning.

Mosby resented the change in his routine. He meowed at the hasty way she set down his dish. He felt restless and cranky. Ever since that bright flash, things hadn't been the same. Mosby whined. Jan heard his complaints. It just couldn't be

"His claws kneaded in and out as he purred with pleasure."

helped. She felt pulled two ways. She was sad and guilty at leaving her cat and joyous about her future. Life was certainly perplexing!

And then the day came. Jan typed her last letter, emptied her desk, showed the new cat feeders Mosby's routine and thanked them for taking over. Then she went down and said goodbye to Ed, leaving him the names of Mosby's caretakers, along with a reminder of his preferences:

"Mosby, the cat, likes: dry cat food, cottage cheese, tuna, milk and hamburgers." She didn't know about the parties. She didn't know he was partial—one might even say addicted—to caviar and lobster, whenever the opportunity arose to indulge in such delicacies.

As a surprise for their last night, and farewell to the Kennedy Center, the young man took Jan to the ballet, Swan Lake. The music lifted their hearts as the swans glided around the stage. The flowing movement of the dancers seemed to create the music.

Mosby was watching from his cozy perch in the ceiling. Something about this music always fascinated him—he never went to sleep during this ballet! His claws kneaded in and out as he purred with pleasure.

After the ballet was over, Mosby went up to his window in his Hideout, as usual. His eyes followed the moving lights, a jet's winking descent, the cars streaming across the bridges, the stars that pricked his night sky.

Then he heard something and slipped into the shadows. No one came to his place at night, but there was someone coming now. The fire door closed softly. Two sets of footsteps hesitatingly felt their way up through the darkness. There were whispers and a muffled giggle. The light barely showed two figures climbing the steps. Mosby could see it was Jan and her young man. They made their way up to the ledge. The young man held out his hand to Jan.

"Here we are," he whispered. He took out his handkerchief, dusted off the chair and gestured for Jan to sit down. She settled herself carefully. He brought out a candle and set it on the crate. The faint hiss of a match lit up his face. A moment later, the lighted candle sent long black shadows dancing behind the two figures on the ledge.

Mosby was dazzled. He had never seen a flame so close before. His eyes glittered in the darkness. The young man brought out two glasses and a small bottle.

"Ta-ta-ta-Ta!" he said with a flourish. Jan smiled as he filled the glasses and gave one to her.

"To us," he said softly. They touched glasses and sipped the wine.

"Oh," said the young man, "here's a little something I bought for Mosby." He brought out a small tin and started unwinding the top. "Sort of a good-bye present. Sardines. Imported." He set them down on the ledge.

Jan managed a shaky smile.

"To Mosby," she said, raising her glass. "Good luck." She drained her glass, then cracked it on the ledge beside her. It broke with a small tinkle.

The young man paused a second, emptied his glass, then tossed it over the edge into the dark. There was a long pause, then the small sound of breaking glass far below. The young man cleared his throat.

"He'll be all right, Jan. Don't you worry; your friends promised to feed him . . ."

Jan turned away and brushed her eyes impatiently. She peered into the shadows, just as she had done that first time.

"Mosby?" There was no sound.

The young man picked up the candle. "He's probably off prowling somewhere," he said. "Come on, let's go."

Together they felt their way down the ladder, down the tier

"He sat staring out the window, motionless."

of cement steps into the darkness below. Mosby watched the light flickering downward.

At the fire door, Jan paused and looked up. Her voice sounded very small and far away.

"Mosby? Good-bye."

The door slammed shut. The flame was gone. Somehow Mosby's Hideout seemed quite dark, lonelier than ever before. He didn't look at the sardines. He sat staring out the window, motionless.

8

Trouble

J an had gone to the other side of the glass. She had
crossed over into the world where people DID things instead of just looked on. At first, when she didn't show up,
Mosby was annoyed. He was still fed daily, but by strangers.
A couple of writers from the American Film Institute volunteered to bring him his food. The fire door in their office
opened into Mosby's Hideout in the unfinished theater. They
usually left a dish of sardines or real cat food on the floor,
just inside the door. But it wasn't the same. Each day, he
sniffed the dish hopefully—there was no familiar scent, no
sign of his friend.

After a few days, a pain began to grow inside him—a pain
like the one he felt when his mother disappeared so long ago.
Then he had mewed his kitten grief. Now this new pain was too
much for a grown tomcat to contain. Mosby howled. He paced
his Hideout and howled. The sound of his loneliness rolled out,

echoing through the vents. Secretaries in the offices nearby listened, their flashing fingers stilled by the sound.

The building manager heard about the cat noises only too soon. He called the A.F.I. offices to make sure Mosby's feeders were on the job. They were.

"He's fed every morning," one of them assured Ed, "just the way Jan said to do it. But he's not eating. I guess he misses her. That's some sound he makes." Even over the phone, the howl of a tomcat was all too clear.

Ed hung up. Now what? He winced, remembering his words to Jan: "It won't matter to him who feeds him . . ." How could he have guessed the cat would howl so?

That afternoon, Mosby crouched in his place in the theater ceiling, waiting for a pause in the talk on stage. In the silence, his long, lonely howls frightened both audience and actors at the matinee.

The people in the audience thought the noise was a part of the play.

"That was a real, live cat!"

"Sure seemed like one."

"How do you think they train it to yell at the right time?"

Mosby howled again.

"Sounds like they're torturing it!"

"Don't be silly. It's just part of the play."

The actors knew those catcalls were not a part of the play. The leading lady was so upset, she refused to go on with the next act until they released the cat trapped in the walls. They called in Ed, who was just leaving for home. He rushed backstage to reassure the actress.

"We know about the cat. You see, he . . . he lives here." The actress was even more upset.

"Lives here? Don't you know cats are unlucky in the theater? LIVES here!"

Ed was embarrassed. It did sound kind of funny.

"You see, he's wild. He's up over the ceiling . . ."

The actress was even more outraged. "I knew it! Trapped in the ceiling! Get it out. I simply refuse to go on until you . . ."

"Dear lady, he is not trapped." Ed wished Mosby WERE trapped! Oh, how he longed to get his hands on that cat! Ed looked at the actress. He could see she was really very upset. He took a deep breath and tried again.

"Don't worry about the cat." He tried to keep his voice calm and reassuring. "He is just an old stray . . . a wild cat that somehow got into the building. He hides out in an unfinished theater on the top floor."

"Why don't you catch him and get him out of there?"

"We can't catch him. He's completely wild."

"He must be starving!"

"No, no, he's fed every day. He really is a very well fed cat! We just can't catch him, that's all."

The actress suddenly smiled. Clearly, this man was as concerned as she was. Her eyes started to twinkle. She realized the whole Kennedy Center was being disrupted by one noisy cat. She nodded.

"I see! You've got yourself quite a problem!" She started powdering her nose and touching up her make-up. She looked at Ed in the mirror.

"I'll go on with the play, but you'd better figure out a way to quiet the cat. He's a hard act to compete with!"

Ed went back to his office. He started to doodle. What could he do? His pencil drew in the long, flat lines of the Kennedy Center roof and balconies.

This job of his demanded so much, even without Mosby, hundreds of problems to face every day. He penciled the columns and windows in a sort of cage grillwork. Then he drew the head of a giant cat, mouth wide, yowling, about to swallow the Kennedy Center!

About this time, the Chairman, Roger, who had only read

about Mosby in the papers, heard Mosby himself, in person. Mosby had discovered that if he howled in an air conditioning vent in his Hideout, the metal pipe echoed, rather like singing in a shower, giving his voice added depth. It sounded like a man he had heard in the Opera House. Mosby began to enjoy his own concerts. But for some reason, Roger didn't. Suddenly, the whole operation of the Kennedy Center was being thrown into chaos by one invisible cat, yowling through a vent that connected, among other places, with the Chairman's office.

Roger picked up the phone. This was a job for his trusted Building Manager, Ed. The conversation went something like this:

Roger: "About this cat . . ."

Ed: "Yes, sir?"

Roger: "He's yowling!"

Ed: "Yes, I heard him." Ed started blacking in the cat's mouth, leaving white fangs.

Roger (through clenched teeth): "Other people have heard him, too."

Ed: "Yes, I can imagine . . ."

Roger: "What's the matter with the dumb cat, anyway?"

Ed: "The person who was feeding him left. A couple of those film people are feeding him. But he won't eat. He misses her, I guess. He . . . you know . . ."

"YOWLS!" said Roger. There was a long silence. Then Roger said, "Ed, I'm putting out a contract to remove that cat! Don't tell me how you do it, just do it. Catch him! Trap him! GET RID OF THAT CAT!"

Ed: "Yes, sir."

Ed hung up the phone. Slowly his pencil blacked out the whole cat!

Mosby was in mortal danger. But at that moment, into Roger's office and into Mosby's life came a willowy lady with a sweet face and a gentle manner. From his under-the-table vantage at VIP parties, Mosby had seen her. But he never knew it was this soft-spoken lady who was to save him. She was Roger's wife, Christine. It also happened that as head of a group of animal lovers called The Animal Welfare Institute, she had made a career of helping all creatures in distress.

"No," said the lady, her voice as bright as a sword. "We must not harm the cat. We must catch him with a humane trap."

"But, Christine . . ."

"You must not harm him." The voice was firm.

Roger suddenly had a feeling he was the one who was trapped. He must save this cat. If he didn't, what would news people say? He could see the headlines already: KENNEDY CENTER HATES CATS!! He didn't hate cats. Not at all. It was just . . . Roger sighed and nodded to his wife.

"All right. We'll trap him . . . HUMANELY!"

And so, late that afternoon, a man from the Humane Society delivered a trap to the Kennedy Center's service entrance, right outside Ed's office. Ed and the man took the trap up by the freight elevator, through the elevator door and into Mosby's Hideout.

Mosby, who had been napping in his window, heard their footsteps and retreated into a dark corner to watch them. They put the trap down near Mosby's eating place. They bent over it, and the man showed Ed how to set it, carefully pulling back the trigger that would spring the trap.

"You see, when the cat's hungry . . . Zing! This thing will slam the door . . ." The door slammed down. Mosby jumped; so did Ed.

"And in the trap will be one very surprised cat." Ed smiled.

"Got the bait?" asked the man. Ed unwrapped a small package. "Hamburger. Very good," said the man. Carefully, they pulled back the spring and laid the hamburger there inside the trap, where the slightest touch would slam the door shut.

"That ought to do it," Ed muttered. "Thanks a lot."

Mosby listened as their footsteps echoed across the floor. Faintly, he heard the clang of the freight elevator door. The elevator hummed, then stopped. Darkness descended on Mosby's Hideout. It was raining, splashing on the marble terrace outside his window. He could hear dripping on his floor in uneven rhythms from the leaks high up in his roof. He was filled with a great sadness. He knew about traps. He had seen many times what they did to a mouse or a rat. He prowled round and round this trap, trying to figure it out.

He was hungry.

9

The Trap

Early the next morning, Ed took the freight elevator up to Mosby's Hideout. Ed was curious to see this cat, which had somehow become entangled in his life. Eagerly he pushed open the fire door. He had expected to hear frantic cries and scramblings. But everything was quiet. Ed was concerned. He hoped nothing had happened to the cat—Roger's wife wouldn't like that! In the gray light, it was hard to see. Ed groped his way over to the trap and peered in.

It was empty.

He checked the bait.

Gone!

The trigger was so delicate, a feather could trip it. The trap was still set, but the hamburger was gone.

"Some cat!" Ed whistled in admiration. Then he sighed. He had been so sure he would catch the cat, he'd brought no more food. So down he went to his underground office, returning with some sardines he'd been saving for a snack for himself. He baited and set the trap again.

"I'll get you this time," he muttered. "See how you like that, cat—that's all the food you're going to get today. No more snacks from the office crowd. I've put a stop to that. You'd better give up, so I can get on with my work."

Ed hurried off, already late for his job. This dumb cat was becoming a darn nuisance!

From the shadows, Mosby watched Ed leave. What was going on now?

Once again, he checked the trap warily. His nose already told him: sardines, one of his favorite foods! He moved around the trap, his tail twitching impatiently. He was still hungry. He ran over to the corner where the new people usually plunked down his dish. There was nothing there. He bounded up to the window ledge. He could still detect the faintest scent of that person who used to come every day, the person with the light step, the soft voice. Her scent was fading; his memory of her was getting blurry, too. Mosby meowed half-heartedly, then went back down to the trap.

The easy life he had enjoyed, Jan's feeding and love, had not spoiled Mosby's wild ways. Thieves never really lose their delicate touch. Carefully and slowly, a gray paw stretched for the sardines. . . .

*　　　　*　　　　*

It was a hard week for everyone.

Every morning, Ed peered into the trap hoping to see, at long last, the wild and invisible cat. As each day passed, his disappointment and admiration grew. Roger waited for the good news that the cat had been caught. He waited in vain. There was no phone call. There was a catcall now and then, but no phone call. Christine waited and worried, afraid, somehow, that Mosby might be hurt.

For Mosby, the center of all the concern, it wasn't easy, either. Trap stealing for food was getting to be a bore.

Fortunately, there was a big party for some important people at the Center that week. The first "guest" carried off half a chicken to dine at leisure while looking out at his favorite view. These parties were great, but Mosby couldn't count on them regularly. And the morsels left in the trap were too small for the big, shining cat Mosby had become. His pain at the loss of Jan was getting confused with hunger pains. His howls of loneliness were becoming howls of hungriness!

At the end of the week, Ed went reluctantly to the Chairman's office to report on the progress of the Trapping of the Cat. Christine was there. She and Roger looked expectantly at Ed. They saw in his face that their plan had failed.

"No luck?"

Ed shook his head.

"I'm sorry, sir. We're up against a real pro. Somehow that cat manages to steal the bait without any trouble."

Wonder and admiration showed in Ed's voice. His eyes sparkled behind his glasses even as he tried to keep his face solemn. Roger sighed.

"This situation is intolerable! What do we do now?"

"We can feed the cat and keep him happy!" It was Christine speaking. She had been waiting anxiously for news that the cat had been caught. She had hoped, like Jan, to take him home. But if he couldn't be caught, there was only one solution.

"If he can't be caught, we must feed him and keep him happy," she repeated.

"What?" If Roger seemed a bit abrupt, it was because chairmen are only human, too. "What about his infernal yowling?"

"Fortunately there was a big party for some important people."

Christine said softly, "If he is fed every day the way that secretary . . . what was her name?"

"Jan," Ed reminded her.

". . . Jan, yes. If we feed him every day the way Jan did, he'll soon settle down." She looked at Ed.

Ed smiled at her and shrugged and wished he were back in his office. "He might settle down. . . ."

"What makes you so sure?"

Christine's voice was soothing. "We can try . . ."

Roger looked at Ed, who was studying his nails.

"I don't see anything else we CAN do, under the circumstances," Ed said, finally. "Feed him and hope he settles down. . . ."

Roger sighed again. "All right. Who will we get to feed him? He wouldn't eat for those people who took over for Jan. . . ." His voice stopped. The room was very quiet. Ed looked up. Both Roger and Christine were looking at him. Ed paused for only an instant, then nodded. "O.K. I'll do it."

Roger smiled apologetically.

"There's really no one else we'd trust. And you ARE here pretty early. . . ."

"Six A.M."

"You'll do it then? You'll feed the cat?" asked Christine.

Ed nodded again. "I hope it works."

"It's got to work," said Christine. "Do you know what he likes to eat?"

"Jan left a list with me," said Ed. "It's in my files."

Christine paused. "She must have been very fond of that cat." Then she added firmly, "Well, we will take care of him now. Won't we?"

And so it was decided. As Ed was leaving, Roger shook his hand.

"I really appreciate this, Ed. I mean, what would people say if they found out we were feeding a wild cat in the top of the Kennedy Center?"

65

*   *   *

There is an organization known as the Friends of the Kennedy Center, "Friends" for short. The Friends, mostly ladies, do all sorts of things—raise money, support the Center, guide tourists, point out all the art work different countries have donated and organize those parties for ambassadors, politicians, all sorts of VIPs—including Mosby.

Now there soon developed another organization, a secret one known to only a few: the Friends of the Kennedy Center Cat, "Catfriends" for short. One of the Catfriends, a lady named Ceci, volunteered to deliver to Ed's office once a month cat food, kitty litter, vitamins, milk, meat and vegetables—all the things essential to cat health. The rest was up to Ed.

The day after the conversation in Roger's office, as Mosby watched, the trap was taken out of his Hideout. The same man who had baited it began coming every morning. He brought dishes of food and fresh water. After a while, Mosby adjusted to the new routine. Gradually, the ache for his lost friend slipped into that special place where fondest memories are stored. He had a new friend now. Of course, it wasn't quite the same. Ed never climbed up to the ledge, or sat and talked to Mosby; he was much too busy for that. But, Mosby understood, here was a man he could trust. It was comforting. He stopped howling.

The Kennedy Center returned to normal.

10

The "Friend"

Well, almost normal. A few weeks later, there was a morning everyone near Mosby's Hideout would long remember. You see, the Catfriends decided Mosby must be lonely. All alone all day and night, day after day, month after month, with no one, no other of his kind to talk to. They thought such a life was quite unnatural.

They agreed he should have a friend—a wife, even! They selected a very pretty, white female cat from the Animal Rescue League. They forgot that even with the best intentions in the world, no one has ever been able to pick out a friend for someone else, let alone a wife.

One morning, as Mosby was enjoying his after-breakfast wash in his window, he heard the freight elevator start its hum. This was not unusual—that elevator hummed up and down all day. But except for Ed's early morning visit with food, it seldom came up to the top floor. This morning, it did.

As he heard the elevator door open, Mosby yawned, stretched and melted down into the shadows to see what was happening. It was Ed, all right, carrying a box. A lady walked beside him with quick steps.

"That's interesting, coming up the back way," she said.

"We had to. No one must know about this," said Ed.

"So this is where he lives!" The lady was looking around, gazing up at the far-away ceiling. It was Ceci.

"Yes, Ma'am, this is his Hideout."

Ceci peered into the shadows. "Do you think he's here? It's so dark. . . ."

"He's around somewhere," said Ed. "He's watching us, all right."

Ceci shivered. "It's such a big and empty place! You know he MUST be lonely all by himself . . . in this . . . this gloomy place."

"I don't know. . . ." Ed shook his head. "He seems to like it."

"Well, I just can't bear to think of him all alone. It's not natural. He needs companionship."

Ed set down the box with a sigh. "I don't know. . . ." He shook his head. "I'm not so sure this is a good idea. If the Chairman should ever find out. . . ."

"How could he ever know? Don't worry—everything is going to be all right from now on!"

"Well, I hope so," said Ed. "I sure hope so." He undid the twine holding the box. "I'll just open this thing a crack."

Ceci peered into the carton. "She looks pretty scared."

"She sure does."

"Come on," Ceci said brightly. "We'd better leave them alone to get acquainted."

Their footsteps died away. The elevator's hum grew fainter and stopped.

Mosby was cautiously curious. What had they brought now? It didn't look like another trap. His eyes, those magical cats eyes that saw clearly even in this dim light, studied the carton. His nose twitched; his ears tuned in on a slight scratching noise. There was something inside the box, something alive. His nose picked up a scent. What was it? There was something familiar about it, some memory of long ago. In a brief flashback, he remembered another carton and warm familiar bodies. He started to circle the box slowly.

Suddenly, he stopped, stunned. There, peering uncertainly out of the box, was a small, white cat!

Now, even the friendliest cat doesn't like a stranger butting in on his home territory. Mosby hadn't seen one of his own kind since he was a kitten. He'd lived alone too long. To him, this small white creature trembling in the carton was not, at last, a friend. It was a Threat! An Invader! An Alien!

Mosby couldn't help himself. His whole being vibrated. The hair on his back rose straight up, like a scrubbing brush. His ears flattened close to his head. His lips curled back in a fierce snarl. He hissed. The little cat crouched, trembling, and tried to hiss back, but she made no sound. Mosby's body arched. His tail grew to twice its normal size. A growl started deep in his throat. He stalked toward this Enemy, moving sideways so he looked even bigger. He was a terrifying sight!

The white cat may have been small and scared, but she had been in tough spots before. She was a stray from the city streets, where survival depended on speed and wits. Here in this strange place, with a terrible, gray, giant of a cat stalking her, every sense was alert, every muscle tensed ready to spring. She crept out of the box, showing her teeth, never taking her eyes off Mosby, but scanning the territory for an escape route. She screamed.

"He stalked this enemy moving sideways so he looked even bigger."

There is something bone chilling, primeval, about a cat's scream. How those long-ago cave people huddled around the fire in the cold night must have trembled at the sound! This scream was an echo of those far-off times.

The workers in the offices had heard Mosby yowl before, but this was different. A hush spread down the hall of desks as every ear and eye turned toward the sound. Mosby screamed in answer as he leapt high to pounce on the enemy.

The little cat did not even pause. She leapt deftly sideways and fled. The chase was on.

Round and round Mosby's Hideout they raced. Up the cement steps, along the ledge, by his window, up over the jutting beams, down again into the shadows, Mosby screaming his rage, the little white cat running for her life. She was fit and swift from her life on the streets; Mosby, confined to his Hideout and his vents and passages, was no match for her speed. He couldn't catch her. Down on the dusty theater floor, she glimpsed a small hole under a door and streaked out into the A.F.I. offices. Mosby didn't follow. He knew there were people out there. He sniffed at the hole and let out one last terrifying cry. In the silence that followed, a film writer giggled nervously. Then everyone started talking at once.

"Did you hear that!"

"What the devil is going on?"

"Call the building manager!"

Someone had already called him. Ed arrived soon afterward and coaxed the little white cat out of the corner behind the drinking fountain. He cuddled the trembling bundle of fur in his arms, stroking her gently.

"I had a feeling this wasn't going to work," he said apologetically. "That Mosby, he's too set in his ways."

So Ed took Mosby's "companion" away. Neither Ed nor the Catfriends ever mentioned their little experiment in friendly relations. When the Chairman heard about that wild morning, he shook his head and kept his thoughts to himself. From that time on, Mosby was left to enjoy his kingdom alone.

11

Mosby Settles Down

I t took a while before Mosby was convinced the Terrible Threat to his territory had really gone. A few nights later, he cautiously approached the hole where the white cat had disappeared. He poked his head through and sniffed the air. There was no alien scent. Carefully, he crept into the office. He had never dared come here before. He paused. There was a hum from the water cooler and a buzz from a night-light at the end of the long room, but no other sound. He prowled down a narrow, flowered carpet between rows of desks. There was no sign of the white cat.

Mosby relaxed. He sharpened his claws on the carpet. A large plant with long, green leaves was growing in a pot beside one desk. Something drew him toward it—the smell of the damp earth, of the leaves. Perhaps it was a feeling for the world of nature that he had never known. He rubbed his head against the side of the pot and inhaled the tangy odor. He closed his eyes.

When he opened them again, yawning and stretching—he froze. Something moved! Down the hall by the drinking fountain, something had moved. Mosby's heart pounded. Facing him, just barely visible in the shadows, was a large gray cat, its eyes glittering fiercely. Mosby's own eyes burned with anger. This was no small, white cat this time, but a large, awesome creature.

Mosby hissed. The gray cat hissed back, silently. Mosby growled and began to stalk this new enemy. The Gray came straight for him, looking terrible and unafraid. The two cats drew closer and closer, growling and hissing, hair electric, tails high. Their piercing eyes, never wavering, seemed to burn like tiny suns. They were frighteningly close.

Head low, ears back, Mosby lashed out, his claws stretched to their fullest. The Gray, copying his every move, lashed out at the same moment. Their paws met! But instead of digging into soft fur, Mosby's paw slid over something hard and cold. He jumped back, then struck again. Again his claws met a slippery surface.

What was this? Mosby sniffed; the strange cat sniffed, too. This cat had no scent! Mosby felt the surface.

Glass!

He knew about windows. But where had this cat come from? Why was he up here behind a window? Mosby tried to find a way around the glass, but met only solid wall and another closed door. He peeked out to see what the other cat was doing, just as the Gray peeked around at him. He leapt in the air, the other cat leapt, too. He hid under a desk, his tail swishing back and forth, then pounced out and ran sideways toward the other cat. They leapt high together and landed facing each other, ever so still.

Somewhere, in this midnight ballet, Mosby's fear disappeared. With that mysterious understanding, he realized, as all cats have since they first bumped into mirrors, that he was

"Somewhere in this midnight ballet—Mosby realized he was dancing with his other self."

dancing with his other self. He sat down and washed. So did the big Gray. He went back and curled up under the plant. The other cat did the same. They looked at each other admiringly. Mosby started to purr. Here was no alien, no threat, but perhaps, somehow, a friend.

After that, in the late night hours, Mosby started sleeping beside the plant, close to the damp earth-smell. The flowered carpet stretched ahead of him to meet the carpet on the other side of the mirror, where his image slept. As time passed, the carpet by the plant grew worn and a circle of cat hairs gave away his favorite nightspot, although no one ever actually saw him sleeping there.

As Mosby's life settled back into a routine, his good spirits and sense of humor blossomed. He invented his own ways of amusing himself. He was alone, but he wasn't lonely.

After midnight, when the building was almost deserted, he liked to play pounce, the game he had learned as a kitten. Suddenly, out of nowhere, he would leap at the night watchmen or the janitors vacuuming the great empty halls. The higher they jumped, the better the game. He raced away to catch them around the next corner. Then, as suddenly as he had appeared, he melted into the walls, to wait until the janitors left before he curled up beside his plant.

When the hum of the elevator announced Ed's arrival with breakfast, Mosby always headed back to his Hideout. He listened as Ed's footsteps crossed the shadowy theater floor, watched as the tall, familiar figure stooped down to pour fresh water and replace yesterday's dish with a clean one full of food. Ed never said much except, "There y'are fella!" Then he hurried off.

*　　　　*　　　　*

Like all cats, Mosby was a creature of habit. His inner clock ran, not by seconds ticking off the time, but by the happenings

"From his sleeping place he could scan the whole office in the mirror."

of his day and night—half-past feeding time, time to nap again—the kind of time most natural to animals and children. Mosby liked his routine, especially the naps.

His day was a series of them. There was the morning nap, just after his after breakfast wash. He settled himself on his ledge, his feet tucked neatly under his chest, and dozed—as motionless as a stuffed cat, except for his ever-listening ears. Occasionally, he squinted drowsily at the tourists wandering by on the terrace outside. He now realized they couldn't see him, even when they shielded their eyes and peered in the dusty window. So, with a great toothy yawn, he would curl up for another nap.

At noon, he went down to his dish for a drink of water and a munch of cat chow—unless, of course, the clatter of dishes announced a tasty people-luncheon. Unknown to the Cat-friends, Henri, the banquet manager, was still trying to catch the thief. He never succeeded.

After lunch, Mosby usually was overcome with sleepiness, and he basked in the afternoon sun streaming in his window until sunset aroused him.

With the setting sun, something stirred inside him, a signal turned on from ages past. "Time for hunting," it said. He grew restless. He would rise, yawn and stretch, front legs, back legs, every muscle and tendon flexed—neck, jaw, back, claw—ready for the night's hunting. He had a favorite beam where he sharpened his claws. Then he trotted off to see what was up in his world.

Evenings at the Kennedy Center are exciting. The building is alive with lights, noise, bustle; the parking lots fill; the restaurants are busy; the people swarm in, eager to be entertained. Mosby didn't go near the Concert Hall. Symphonies tended to put him to sleep (as they do some humans). There was something about the sound of those violin strings that made him nervous. But he always dropped in to check the latest offering in the theaters, occasionally showing his pleasure with a well-timed howl of approval. His fame was spreading through the theater world. The actors had become used to his occasional "ad-libs." They decided he was good luck.

Mosby never interrupted the ballet. It was his favorite entertainment. This wordless mixture of music and motion is certainly most suited to the cat—although cats must dance out their feelings in silence.

Now that Mosby was contented, most people forgot about him. But not Christine. She still hoped someday to catch the cat and bring him home.

Not Jan, far away in Philadelphia. Sometimes in the evenings as she sat by the fire and stroked the kitten curled in her lap, her face would grow soft and sad—remembering Mosby, she hoped he was all right.

Not the Chairman, Roger. He still was worried, knowing that Mosby was still somewhere in his building, ready to express his feelings if things didn't suit him precisely.

Not Ceci, who faithfully bought Mosby's supplies.

And certainly not Ed. He even came in on weekends to be sure Mosby was well fed. And much to his wife's annoyance, Ed never took a vacation. He felt he couldn't. That cat really counted on him.

So the seasons came and went. The Kennedy Center grew and prospered. And so did the Kennedy Center Cat.

And then, one morning, it happened.

12

Disaster

In the pre-dawn silence, Mosby dozed, floating in that state reserved for cats and mothers of small children—halfway between awake and asleep. Only the tip of his tail twitched, and his ears moved slowly, like antennae. This was the quietest time. There was just the faintest humming, as if his building snored ever so gently. No sounds of the waking city penetrated the vast, soundproof structure. No daylight reached the windowless corridor of the A.F.I. offices. But Mosby's inner clock told him it was about That Time.

He opened one eye, lazily. From his sleeping place on the carpet under his plant, he could scan the whole office in the mirror. He could see if anyone tried to sneak up behind him. He could also watch the magnificent Gray on the other side of the glass. Mosby yawned, admiring the white fangs and bright pink tongue of his other self.

Far off, he heard the hum of the elevator. He rose, stretched, and drifted behind the desks, over the sill into the safer darkness of his Hideout. He knew it was the Man bringing food, but out of habit he hid to watch him come.

Ed's familiar stride echoed down the hall. Mosby was leaning forward, poised in anticipation of his breakfast, when—

CRASH!!

Ed tripped over the sill and staggered into the wall just beyond. The noise sent Mosby flying into the darkest corner. How he hated loud noises!

Ed leaned against the wall for a moment, recovering from the shock of almost falling.

"That was sure clumsy," he told himself. "I've stepped over that sill a thousand times." His elbow hurt where he had smashed into the wall. Then he noticed he was still clutching the jar of water and the cat dish.

"Didn't spill a drop!" Ed muttered in amazement, but then whistled as a pain shot up his leg.

"Oh boy, I must have sprained something!"

By trying to save the water jug from breaking, Ed had spun around, landing heavily on one foot, twisting it under him. He limped across the floor, groaning as he bent to exchange dishes and pour out fresh water. He straightened up carefully and managed to grunt through clenched teeth, "There y'are, fella." His hand groped for the wall and he stood uncertainly, as if suddenly he didn't feel like moving.

This was the first time the Man had not hurried off. Mosby waited, watching. Ed looked around.

"I hope I didn't scare you, cat." He flexed his foot. "Whew," he whispered, sucking air through his teeth and biting his lip. He peered into the shadows and called in a pained voice, "Mosby? You ARE here, aren't you? Mosby?"

Before he thought, Mosby answered with a cheerful chirp. Ed's eyeglasses sparkled as he caught the flash of cat's eyes in the shadows near him.

"Hey, there!" he said softly.

Just as if he did it every day, Mosby strolled out, arching his back and rubbed against Ed's leg. Ed stood stone still. For the second time in his life, Mosby, of his own free will, had come close to a person. He rubbed against Ed again, then trotted over to his food. Ed stared hard. At last, there before him, was this untrappable, invisible cat! He remembered Jan's story of her first glimpse, long ago. He blinked his eyes. It was hard to see in this light, but Mosby was handsome, all right, fat and shining.

Ed sighed. It was time to get to work. He tested his sore foot, putting his weight down carefully. He frowned and whispered, "Ow!"

Mosby watched Ed stagger to the doorway, his footsteps making a queer uneven rhythm—step-STEP, step-STEP—then, as the man disappeared, he bent over his dish again, growling with pleasure. The man had put in some chicken livers, a rare treat.

As usual, Mosby followed his meal with a morning wash-up in his window. (Happy cats wash a lot.) He spent that day in his nappish way, quite unaware of the problem building up like a giant thunderhead on his horizon.

Ed made it down to his office—just. He hobbled in and sank down in his chair. His secretary breezed in at 8:30, singing, "Good morning," as she started to water her plants. There was no answering greeting from her boss, but this was not unusual. He was often absorbed in some problem. So she finished her chores, then brought Ed a fresh cup of coffee. He was still bent over his desk, his head in his hands.

"Something wrong?" she asked.

Ed looked up. Like many people who have hurt themselves, he felt stupid. He smiled at her, weakly.

"What's the matter?" she asked.

"Matter? Oh, ah, yes, I think I've hurt my leg," said Ed.

"Your leg? How?"

His leg hurt so, it was hard to concentrate.

". . . Mosby strolled out, arching his back and rubbed against Ed's leg."

"Um, well, you see, I sort of tripped when I went up to feed the cat this morning."

"Oh, that cat!" The secretary thought the whole cat business was foolish. "All this time spent on a dumb stray—well! When you think of all the people starving. . . ."

Ed looked at her and looked away. He knew what she meant. There were many others who felt the same way. He sighed and started to stretch his foot. He winced. She noticed his pale face and was suddenly very concerned.

"You really are hurt!"

"Just turned my ankle, or something."

"Here, let's see."

Ed was embarrassed, but spun his chair around and pulled up his trouser, shyly. His ankle was swollen above the tight shoe. It looked awful.

"I think you've broken something! You'd better see a doctor."

So Ed was sent away for X-rays. He was almost relieved to find he really HAD broken something—about twenty bones in his foot. They wrapped his leg in a heavy cast. The doctor's instructions were firm as he spoke to Ed's wife, who had come to drive him home. Funny how doctors treat a patient, not looking at him, talking over his head.

"He must not walk on that foot. No stairs."

"How long will it be before he can climb stairs?" asked Ed's wife.

The sentence rang in Ed's ears: "Two months."

Ed's wife was delighted. Now, at last, he would have that vacation she'd been looking forward to.

She should have known better. Ed was at work the next day, as usual—but with his leg in its cast, propped up on a drawer. He had too many problems, and no one who quite understood. The first problem was: who would feed the cat?

13

Mosby Howls Again

Mosby was waiting for breakfast. The elevator was late. He paced up and down, letting out impatient meows. The lean stray who had searched over trash for a sparse meal was now a demanding king of his domain. He had become accustomed to prompt service. He meowed again. Where was breakfast?

It was on its way. The elevator finally started to hum. But when Mosby heard the footsteps, he crouched down. This was not Ed.

A stranger—a short, fat figure—stepped over the sill and made his way across the floor. He was muttering, "As if I didn't have enough to do! I've got to take time to come up here to this godforsaken spot to feed some no-count cat!"

He put down a dish with a crash and stomped out. Mosby's skin twitched. He sniffed the dish. It was unwashed and smelled sour. The sour scent of the strange man was on it.

Where was Ed? Where was his fresh water? What was going on? That first day Mosby didn't eat. He circled his dish once. He peed nearby to show his disgust. Then he went and sulked in his window.

Remembering Mosby's performance after Jan left, Ed was apprehensive. He'd given the chore of feeding the cat to a maintenance man, told him exactly what to do and where to go, and hoped everything would be all right. He was relieved when no complaints of catcalls came into his office.

His relief was premature. Mosby's sulks soon built up into a giant-size rage. He hadn't done it in a long time, but he did it again now—he howled.

A bit later, the Chairman was having a conference in his office and was polishing last-minute plans for the opening of the new play the next evening. Several members of his committee were gathered to report on the after-theater party. In the middle of a sentence, Ceci came rushing in.

The Chairman glanced up. "Yes?"

"Oh, sorry, I didn't know you were busy."

She knew. But she just had to warn him.

"Could I see you for just a moment? It's about . . ." Ceci tried to signal to Roger by twirling imaginary whiskers.

"Not now, later," said Roger, puzzled by her strange behavior.

"But it's about the . . ." Ceci looked around at the committee members, and paused. "The Gray Ghost! He's calling!"

One of the committee said brightly, "Oh, it's that guessing game. I love it." She leaned forward. "Act it out by syllables!"

Roger looked at Ceci as if she'd gone mad.

The committee lady murmured, "Gray ghost? . . . Gray ghost! That's the Rebel Colonel Mosby!"

Ceci nodded. "Right!" She looked at Roger. Light dawned.

Roger said slowly, "Oh, Mosby . . . yelling?"

"Rebel yell!" shouted the lady. "I win!"

Roger looked at Ceci and pleaded, "He can't be."

"He is."

"Now?"

Ceci nodded. "Ed's on the phone."

Roger, mumbling, picked it up. "One moment ladies . . . Hello, Ed?" He tried to keep his voice calm. "I hear our friend is . . . um . . . tuning up. Yes, well, can't you stop him? Well, just go up there and . . ." Roger listened a moment, then muttered, "What do you mean you can't go up? . . . What ABOUT your foot? . . . Broken!" Roger's voice was suddenly sympathetic.

"Well, Ed, I'm sorry to hear that, of course—I didn't know. How did it happen?" Then a little louder: "You don't mean it! The cat . . .? That infernal . . . Well, how long before you can go up there? . . . Two months! We can't wait two months!"

Roger looked around at the committee members all listening attentively. He smiled at them in what he hoped was a reassuring way.

"Listen, Ed, we're planning a party after the opening performance tomorrow night. So it's very important to . . . to have everything quiet . . . you know what I mean . . . quiet as a cat . . . er, um quieter than that! You simply have to . . . um . . ." Roger looked into the alert faces of the committees and said blandly, "You have to prevent any disturbance!" Then he hung up.

Down in his office, Ed got the message, all right. He had to keep Mosby quiet. But how? His secretary had a suggestion. "Why not call Dr. Michael Fox, that vet who writes a column in the paper. He's supposed to be an animal psychologist. Maybe he will have an idea . . ."

Ed brightened. But when he got Dr. Fox on the phone, he found it a little hard to explain. Roger had insisted that no one mention the Kennedy Center was Mosby's home.

"Dr. Fox? I have a problem. You see, I have this cat." Ed

"When he got Dr. Fox on the phone, he found it a little hard to explain."

gulped. "Well, I don't exactly HAVE him, but I feed him . . . That is, I used to feed him . . . and now I can't."

Ed paused and took a deep breath. "It's hard to explain . . ."

"Yes?" Dr. Fox tried to sound encouraging.

"You see, I can't get to him right now."

"Why?"

"Well, you see, he's . . . um . . . he's up in the . . . um . . . attic."

"Won't come down, eh?"

"No."

"I see your problem."

"That's not the problem," said Ed patiently. "You see, I broke my leg. . . ."

"Sorry to hear that."

". . . So I can't get up there to feed him . . . and he howls."

"Oh, well, that's no problem. He's probably just hungry."

"No, no, I got someone else to feed him, but the cat won't eat. He just howls."

"Well, that's the problem then. He misses you!" said the Doctor, triumphantly.

"I guess so," sighed Ed. "But what can I do? He howls and I've got to stop him. That's my problem. HOW?"

Dr. Fox thought a moment. Then he said, "Try fixing his food yourself, the way he's used to. He will smell your scent on the dish. Maybe that will do it."

"Just that? It seems so simple."

"Sometimes the simple solutions are the best."

"I'll try. Thanks a lot."

Dr. Fox hung up, shaking his head. "That's a weird one. A guy who keeps his cat in the attic!"

But it worked. Ed washed and fixed Mosby's dish himself from then on before sending it up with the maintenance man. Mosby quieted down. No one was exactly sure why. But he stopped howling.

The Chairman's new play was a success, unmarred by cat-calls from above the ceiling. The after-theater party was a sparkle of clinking glasses, bubbling laughter and glowing praise of the play. To some of the guests, Roger seemed inattentive, his head cocked as if listening for some far-off sound. There was no sound—no rude comments from his tenant upstairs. Actually, his tenant was right there enjoying the party—under cover, of course.

*   *   *

Two months is a long time to wait. Mosby was puzzled by the new feeding arrangements. The short stranger who brought his food was always abrupt and grouchy. But Ed's scent was there on the dish every morning. To Mosby's delight, those little extras never failed to appear. So he quieted down and waited.

For Ed, it was a long wait, too. He had never been the sort to put his feet up on his desk. Trying to work with one foot in the air was aggravating. He worried about a lot of things, but especially about the cat. His secretary found more and more memos surrounded by doodles of cats.

And then, at last, the cast came off. Ed's foot felt as if it were full of needles, but he was walking! Next morning Ed was fixing Mosby's dish with special care, when the short little maintenance man grouched in.

"I'll feed the cat myself today," said Ed, trying to sound casual. The grouchy little man smiled for the first time in two months.

"Don't trip over that sill!" he warned, as Ed limped off toward the freight elevator.

Later, when Ed's secretary arrived, she found Ed pacing up and down, practicing walking.

"Fed him myself this morning."

"How was he?" She didn't have to ask who "him" was.

Ed stopped pacing and smiled, remembering.

"You should have seen that cat! He ran out to meet me and went round and round . . ." He sighed and smiled again, broadly. ". . . Rubbing against my legs and purring up a storm!"

The secretary started to make one of her wisecracks, but the look on Ed's face stopped her.

"I put down my hand—not open, mind you. He's still too wild for that. But I showed him the back of my hand and he rubbed against it over and over." Ed rubbed his knuckles, remembering.

"You know, I think that fella was glad to see me!"

14

The Good Life

Aⁿd so Mosby settled down. The days passed, one quite like another. Safe in his private world, Mosby grew fat and contented. Season followed season. He watched it all, the make-believe and the real, not caring which was which.

Summer was the liveliest time. His river was filled with color and motion. In the early mornings and late afternoons, the long, thin sculls with their many oars, like giant water bugs, cut sharp ripples in the still water as they skimmed swiftly by. Sailboats glided from shore to shore; powerboats flew along on their curling bow waves. Fat sightseeing boats moved purposefully up to the distant bridge and turned back, never varying their routine.

People strolled on Mosby's terrace in a colorful, never-ending stream. They gazed at the river view, pausing to hold up their black boxes as if to see it better, then moved on. The children looked wistfully at the river and the empty sand beaches on the distant shore, so inviting, so impossibly far away. They peered in his window, trying to see past the glare of the terrace. They looked until their parents, their eyes deep in the guidebooks, dragged them away.

Some people came by two's, walking slowly, close together, reminding Mosby of something he couldn't quite remember—somehow those two's, hand in hand, made him feel empty. Not hungry for food, but for something—something lost. Then he'd turn from his window and make a sort of lonely cry. He'd pace his place as if somewhere in the shadows he might find the thing he missed.

Just when it seemed this show would go on forever, sunny, bright, busy, there came a change. No wind ruffled his glossy fur, his quivering nose picked up no cold scent of autumn, but still he sensed it. He watched the fall storms move down his sky, great black clouds churning, rocking the incoming jets, turning his river dark and lumpy. Slowly, the summer green of the far shore faded to rust and gold.

Those few people who came to his terrace hurried by, bundled up, leaning against the river wind. The boats stopped coming; logs and leaves from the fall storms floated by. Flocks of ducks rested in the lee of the island and then were gone.

All sorts of birds flew past the window—little groups down low, long V-shaped flights up high—even, one long afternoon, hundreds of orange and black butterflies alternately fluttering and coasting—all headed south. Sometimes a lone bird would land on Mosby's terrace. The bird would be hunched down, breathing fast, its feathers rumpled. Mosby resisted the temptation to pounce. But the whole business made him feel restless. Leaves blew high in the strange winds, some falling to huddle in corners against his window. Everything was stirring, changing—even the sun was losing its warmth, setting low and red against a different part of the shore.

"They peered in his window, trying to see past the glare of the
terrace."

The nights were different, too. The moon, in summer so large and soft, looked far away and hard, the stars brittle.

And then one day, his island was bare; the river steamed; the cars on the bridges steamed; smoke drifted from the chimneys over against the sky. His whole world seemed one cold veil of mist. Winter had come.

Winter was a solitary time. No tourists roamed the empty, leaf-strewn terrace. The river glittered in the slanting sun. Gray patches of ice grew out from the shore. Sometimes snow came, softening the bleakness. Mosby loved the snow. He sat for hours, entranced, watching the dark flakes drift down from the smoke-gray sky.

And, of course, whenever he tired of the outside scene, he turned to the amusements of his building, where everything stayed bright and warm and noisy. He was a faithful first-nighter, watching with interest each new production. Unlike the Chairman, the theater people felt a special thrill when their Good-luck Cat meowed his approval. Inside Mosby's building, there was no change. The red carpets—the crowds moving, laughing, clapping—the sparkling lights, the parties, and the silence when they all went away and he prowled his building alone—all this was forever the same.

His greatest comfort was Ed, his friend who fed him daily. His inside world was changeless and secure.

*   *   *

When life is a routine, time passes fast. It's the unusual times we remember. So it was with Mosby. Spring had come again, and with it the return of life. New leaves covered his island with a haze of green, sprinkled here and there with the whites of flowering trees. The birds and the tourists returned and his river was again alive with boats. The dreary winter scene was only a memory.

It had been five years since his building had been finished, and celebrations came fast. Mosby attended them all. There was the Chairman's birthday, a full-dress affair glittering with VIPs both on the stage and in the audience. Jewels sparkled like ice on ladies' throats and wrists. There were so many acts that Mosby took a small nap. He awoke to the ear-tingling noise of hand clapping, people shouting. Mosby yawned and looked down. There below him, very small and far away, was Roger, the man whose life was so entwined with his. He was trying to say something. He held the curtain, as if for support, and bowed shyly. A lively blonde lady came out and took his hand and started singing, "Hello, Roger, well, hello, Roger . . ."

The people stood and cheered. Mosby added his heartiest yowl to the din. A brief frown crossed Roger's face. Was that a catcall? It couldn't be! Roger looked up towards the ceiling, but the lights blinded him. He wiped his eyes.

A few days later, Roger got the news he'd been hoping for. Smiling, he turned to Christine. "We've done it! We've got the money to finally finish that unfinished theater! The Japanese have given us three million. . . ." He stopped. She didn't look exactly overjoyed. "Christine?"

"What about the cat?" she asked.

"The cat?—the cat!" Roger's eyes rolled heavenward.

"What will happen to Mosby," she persisted, "when they go messing around up there? Roger, we've just got to get him out."

Roger smiled grimly. "I know, I know! I've always wanted to get him out."

"We could get that man who catches wild animals on TV . . ."

"Who?" said Roger.

"You know. They set a net with springs and it flies up and traps the animal . . . then that young man with the muscles runs out and . . ."

"Muscles? What ARE you talking about?"

99

"I'm talking about Mosby," she said patiently. "We could get that wild man from Omaha, you know, on TV . . . We could get him to catch Mosby."

The Chairman frowned. "Now, Christine, we are not going to get a TV wild-animal man up in that empty theater." He stood up. "Don't you worry, we'll think of something. Besides, you know how builders are. It will take forever before they actually start. Why, the cat might die of old age by the time . . ." He stopped. "Just a joke."

That afternoon, when he was alone in his office, Roger called his Building Manager.

"Ed? Good news! We've finally got the money for that little theater. Now we can go ahead and finish it . . . WHOSE place? . . . Oh, yes, Mosby's Place. Well, now we really do have to get that cat out of there . . . He comes when you feed him, doesn't he? . . . Does he let you touch him? . . . Well, why can't you just GRAB him? . . . Sure he might run off, but what have we got to lose? Time is running out. Tomorrow—just grab him."

It was an order. Ed had to try. He drummed on his desk, then buzzed for his secretary. "Get me that doctor, the animal psychologist."

"The one who helped when you broke your foot. . . . Dr. Fox?"

"Yes, that's the one. But be sure not to mention the Kennedy Center."

"I know," sighed the secretary.

Ed started a doodle of a square with a small cat in one corner. He began penciling in the square, black lines closing in on the cat. "Dr. Fox? Yes, this is the Building Manager . . . Uh, this is, well . . . You may not remember me, but you helped me out some time ago. I'm the man who has this cat who lives up in the . . . um . . . attic."

"Yes?"

"He howled when I couldn't feed him when I broke my leg. . . ."

"Yes?" Dr. Fox sounded vague. Then suddenly he said positively, "Yes! The man with the Attic Cat! I remember. Did he stop howling?"

"Yes, yes, it worked perfectly. He is just fine . . ."

"Still lives in the attic?"

"Um . . . yes . . . but I've got a real problem. We're going to be doing some, um, repairs . . . up there, and I've got to get the cat out."

"Well, as I remember, he was very fond of you. What's the trouble?"

"You see, no one has ever picked him up."

"Oh?"

"He's afraid to be touched."

"Oh, yes, that sometimes happens in cats. It's called 'hyperesthesia.' "

"What?"

"A super-sensitivity to touch. Such cats are shy. They hide out of sight."

"That's Mosby," Ed nodded. "He's always been that way."

"Mosby?"

"That's the cat."

"Ah, yes, well . . . maybe he had a fright when he was young."

"Maybe. Anyway, I've just got to catch him and move him out of there. Any suggestions . . .?" Ed asked hopefully.

"A tranquilizer might help," said the doctor.

"I don't want to knock him out. He might run into the vents and disappear . . ."

"I've got a powder. You could put it in his food. It sometimes acts pretty fast, but doesn't last long. . . ."

Ed though a minute, then said, "All right. I'll try it."

"I'm operating this afternoon, so I'll leave the envelope with instructions at the desk. What was the name?"

"Um," Ed hesitated. "Just say . . . for Mosby. I'll pick it up on my way home. Thank you, doctor."

Dr. Fox hung up and frowned. "Something strange about that man. Oh, well, this amount of tranq can't do any harm."

15

Mosby's Fourth

Next day was a day Mosby would never forget—or maybe never remember. It started all wrong. The moment Ed came in with his breakfast, Mosby felt a tenseness in the air. Ed stayed close by, watching the cat eat. He'd never done that before. The food had a strange taste. Even though it was liver, Mosby stopped eating halfway through, shaking his head as if he was suddenly dizzy. He staggered over to Ed as if for comfort and rubbed against the back of his hand. Ed rubbed his knuckles along Mosby's side. He couldn't keep his hand from trembling. Mosby sensed the electricity in the air.

"This isn't going to hurt you now," Ed whispered. "Easy, fella . . ." Then, with a swift motion, he tried to scoop up the cat. When Ed's hand closed on him, Mosby squirmed loose and jumped away as if he'd been burned. He scuttled out of reach and looked over his shoulder. He shook his head as if to clear it. He swayed drunkenly. Ed stayed where he was, kneeling by the dish. "Oh, rats!" he said.

Ed took a deep breath. Then, trying to control his frustration, he whispered, "Come on, fella, I'm not going to hurt you . . ." Mosby washed his back nervously. His skin twitched. His tail swished irritably. Ed waited. But the tranquilizer seemed to have made the cat angry instead of sleepy. Finally, Ed stood up. Mosby ran off a few steps and watched warily. Ed brushed off his knees. "All right . . . I was afraid it wouldn't work." He looked at the cat, a moment ago so friendly. Now Mosby was glaring at him from the shadows. Ed held out his hand. At the gesture, the cat crouched, ready to flee. Ed sighed, turned and walked slowly away.

Mosby stared unseeing at the doorway. He felt peculiar. His ears buzzed. The floor swayed. He dug in his claws to keep from falling. He shook his head to clear it, but the buzzing became a roar. He felt a desperate need to hide. He staggered drunkenly into a dark corner and collapsed. In an instant, he was asleep, snoring gently.

He slept all morning. When he awoke, he felt much better. Hungry and thirsty. He drank from his water bowl, then turned to his unfinished breakfast. He was hungry, but there was something strange about his food. He sniffed at it and turned away. He went up to his window to wash and noticed his terrace was crowded with tourists, many carrying little flags. Something was up. He was sure of it when, sometime later, Ed came in with some security guards to check his Hideout.

That usually meant a party, so Mosby trotted off by his secret route to investigate. Sure enough, tables were being set up in one of the banquet rooms. He waited patiently, watching the waiters arrange the platters of food. He was an old pro. He knew just when to strike. As the last waiter disappeared out the door, he flashed up on the table, surveyed the array of goodies just right for the Discriminating Cat, chose a not-so-dainty morsel and scurried gaily away, his lunch held tight in his teeth, one step ahead of the angry Henri.

He retired to his window to dine in the fading light. After washing up, he watched the sunset. The sky and the river seemed to cling to a last brightness, while the dark crept over the land. Suddenly, above the trees on the far shore, a spray of fire burst in the darkening sky and vanished. Before he could quite believe what he had seen, there came another flash, and another! Mosby was fascinated. Trails of sparks soared upward, as if trying to touch the stars, then flowers of light bloomed and faded downward into darkness. Some were like the shooting stars he sometimes saw at night, only nearer and brighter. Then there were several eye-blinding bursts, bright as suns. He heard no sound, but he felt his building tremble. He started, uneasily.

Just at that moment, the fire door slammed. A clatter of footsteps stopped suddenly. Mosby heard the sound of panting. A cough cut through the darkness. Then a small voice whispered.

"Come on, come on, let's go." There was a pause. "Hurry up. We're gonna miss the whole show!"

"Wait a minute," a low voice interrupted. "I gotta figure this thing out . . ."

"Huh!" a husky voice said angrily. "What you mean is you got us lost."

"Wait a minute. Light a match." There was a scratch. In the faint light of the match Mosby saw three figures at the base of the steps. They looked like three small actors in one of his plays. Their shadows danced away into the darkness of the bottom floor far below.

"This ain't the way to the roof!" whispered the smallest one, peering around with frightened eyes.

"Joe, where are we? You said you knew a back way . . ."

The middle one held the match up high. "Look at there!" All three peered over the edge just as the light went out. "Shoot!" Another match flickered and in its feeble flame, the three leaned over the edge of the abyss, then backed away together.

"This is SOME place!"

105

"I don't like it. Let's go," the small voice whined. "We're going to miss the show, I tell you!"

"Wait a minute. I got an idea." There was a rustling as the middle one pulled some sticks out of a paper bag.

"We'll have our own show right here."

There was a hiss. Suddenly, Mosby saw a magical thing. The stick one of the boys was holding started spraying out stars, little bright stars that arched out and vanished in the dark. It was scary but beautiful.

"Hey, neat! Gimme one," said the small boy.

"Take it easy. I got a whole box." Soon, they each held one of these shining things. The boys started laughing and waving their arms, making a dazzling design of bright lines of light and hissing stars that held them all in its magic. When one died, they lit another and another. Then, finally, there was just one left. It sputtered and went out, leaving a red spot glowing in the dark.

"Boy!" said the small voice, wistfully. "That was neat!" The hoarse voice broke the silence that followed. "Come on, let's go. Someone might catch us . . ."

"Wait," said the low-voiced one. "I've got a couple more surprises."

There was a rustling, and Mosby, like the boys, waited. Up to this point, he, too, had been fascinated by the gently hissing stars. It was as good as any theater performance. So he was quite unprepared for what happened next.

A match flared. Suddenly, a loud and more sinister hissing filled the silence. A trail of red sparks arched out and disappeared over the edge. Then, suddenly, with a burst of flashes, the whole place exploded with noise! Bang after bang met its echoes bouncing off the walls. Mosby scuttled to the nearest corner, where he cowered, trembling, his ears flat, his eyes staring as the waves of noise rushed over him.

Then there was silence. He could hear his heart pounding. There were mumbled voices. He glanced back over his shoul-

"A dazzling design of bright lines of light and hissing stars . . ."

der in time to see a trail of sparks rise up towards the roof then fiery balls burst with an angry, earshattering POW! POW! POW!

It was unbearable. Mosby trembled. His teeth chattered. He panted and drooled. He tried to bury himself in the cement floor of the platform.

As suddenly as it began, the noise stopped. In the silence, the small voice whispered, "Joe, they're gonna catch us for sure! We better get out of here before they . . ."

"Right," said the low voice. "Just this last one for old George and the 200th! This is REAL! Dig it!"

There was the warning hiss, then a tremendous flash and a deafening BANG! Louder than any of the others. Louder than one shaken cat could bear. Mosby went into shock. He didn't hear the nervous giggles, nor the footsteps running and the final bang of the fire door.

He crouched in his corner, shivering uncontrollably. He couldn't move. He just crouched there, panting and shaking, his eyes wide and unseeing.

16

Scared

E d hurried up to Mosby's Hideout the next morning. Ed hadn't slept well. He was anxious about the cat, what with the tranquilizer and trying to grab him and all. He put down the fresh food and waited, but no gray figure trotted out. The place seemed empty.

"I never should have tried to pick him up," he thought. "Now I've scared him." He peered into the shadows where Mosby usually hid. "Fella? Come on out. I won't try it again." There was no sound. He started across the floor, stumbled and then bent over to pick up a funny looking stick lying at his feet. He sniffed—it smelled of something strange. What was it? Suddenly he noticed the same sharp, smoky odor all about him. Gunpowder!

Ed looked around suspiciously. He picked up several burnt-out sticks and a few bent sparkler wires. He poked his foot at a blackened place where it looked as if a whole pack of firecrackers had scorched the floor. Further over was a great, black blast mark—all that was left of what must have been the grand-daddy of all giant crackers.

"Oh, no!" The picture was only too clear. "Oh, poor fella!" Looking around anxiously, Ed called, "Mosby? Are you there?" There was no chirp, no meow, no sound. "It's all right, fella." Silence. "It's going to be all right," he said, as if to reassure himself. But in his heart Ed knew it was all wrong. His bungling attempt to catch the cat was minor compared to what must have happened last night. Slowly and sadly, he left, carrying his armload of burnt-out sticks.

Lately, Ed's secretary had noticed her boss seemed more worried than usual. But this morning, he really looked sick.

"Have a nice Fourth?" she asked, trying to get his mind off his troubles.

"Oh, blast the Fourth!" Ed cried, pounding his desk, startling even himself.

His secretary jumped and spilled the coffee she was bringing. "What's the matter?"

"I'm sorry. Somebody celebrated up in Mosby's Hideout last night. Shot off fireworks all over the place."

"How awful! How do you know . . .?"

"That stuff was all over the floor up there." He pointed to the burnt remains he had thrown in his wastebasket.

"But who . . .? How . . .?"

"Oh, I don't know. Some kids, probably, just sneaked in somehow while everyone was watching the big show at the Monument." He glanced toward the sticks. "Must have made an awful racket—Mosby didn't come for his food this morning." Ed rubbed his forehead. "I wish I could catch those kids!"

"Oh, well, he'll recover," the secretary said, trying to sound cheerful. "I remember when I was little, I hated the Fourth. I used to go hide in the cellar . . ." Her voice trailed off. Ed wasn't listening. "Well, better get to work."

110

Ed doodled a circle round and round. "He hates noise. It must have scared him almost to death."

Ed went up to the Hideout just before he left that afternoon. There was no sign of Mosby. His food was untouched. Same thing the next day. When she came to work, the secretary found her boss staring at nothing, biting his lip. He didn't even doodle.

"No sign of him yet?" she asked. Ed shook his head. "Have you told . . . um . . . anybody?" Ed shook his head. "No need to bother anyone," she said.

Ed shook his head. "Nope." He sighed. "But the Chairman is sure to call. He asked me to get rid of Mosby. Now what can I tell him?"

At that moment the phone rang. It was Roger.

"Hello, Ed. Meant to get back to you. Did you tend to that little business?"

"Hmm?" said Ed.

"Is the cat gone?"

"Um," Ed swallowed hard. "Yes, sir. He's gone."

"You caught him? Good man!" said Roger, his voice bright with relief.

"Well, not exactly . . ." said Ed.

"What do you mean?"

"I mean I didn't catch him. He has just—disappeared."

"How?" Roger wanted to know. "How can the cat just—disappear?"

"Sir, it's a pretty long story . . ." Roger didn't really take it all in, only a few key phrases. "Tranquilizer didn't . . . work . . . kids in the theater . . . fireworks scared him . . . And so you see," said Ed, "he just disappeared. I don't know where."

The phone was silent.

"I hope you find him," said the Chairman finally.

"I hope so, too," said Ed. He hung up the phone.

"Could that tranquilizer have knocked him out?" the secretary asked from the doorway.

Ed shook his head. "That was only supposed to last a few minutes. I keep wondering if he could have been hurt when the fireworks exploded . . ."

"Why not call Dr. Fox. Maybe he'll have some idea."

Ed looked up, his face brightening. "I'll do that."

Ed dialed.

"Dr. Fox? This is the man with the . . . um . . . Attic Cat . . ."

"Oh, yes, did it work? Did you catch your cat?"

"No."

"Sorry."

"The stuff seemed to make him more alert," said Ed.

"Yes, well, tranqs sometimes do that."

"I tried to grab him, but he ran off."

"Too bad," said the doctor.

"I was just wondering if . . . if it could have knocked him out . . ."

"Oh, no, not with the dose I gave you. He should have been fine in a few minutes."

"Well, then I . . . Dr. Fox, I . . . I've got to tell you . . . I'd like to keep this in strictest confidence . . . off the record. You see . . ." Ed paused.

"Yes?"

"You see, I'm the Building Manager of the Kennedy Center . . ."

"Yes?"

"And this cat isn't in MY attic . . . he's in the Kennedy Center attic."

"The . . . WHAT?"

"He's a sort of wild cat who lives up on the top floor of the Kennedy Center."

"Oh, yes! The Kennedy Center Cat! I seem to remember reading about him once. I thought he was gone long ago."

"No, he's still there—at least I think he is. You see, something terrible has happened . . ."

112

"You mean after you tried to catch him?" asked the doctor.

"Yes, someone shot off some fireworks up there."

"Fireworks? In the Kennedy Center!"

"In this unfinished theater . . . where the cat lives . . . you see, it's a tremendous place, three stories high."

"Amazing!"

"Anyway," Ed went on, "it must have scared him."

"I should think so!"

"He hasn't eaten . . ."

"Loss of appetite. Yes, yes, that's to be expected. Cats have extremely sensitive nervous systems. They often overreact to sudden and unexpected stimuli."

"Huh?"

"The noise may have scared him," explained the doctor.

Ed mopped his brow. "That's what I'm trying to tell you."

"Yes, well, are there any other symptoms? Depression? Listlessness? Shivering?"

"I don't know. He's disappeared."

"Disappeared?"

"Vanished. I haven't seen him since it happened."

"Are you sure he hasn't run away?" asked the doctor.

"Oh, no." Ed's voice was certain. "He can't get out of there. The whole top floor is secured by fire doors."

"How long has he been missing?"

"Three days." To Ed, it seemed like forever.

"Hmmm," said Dr. Fox. "Hmmmm!" It was his thinking sound. "Gone into hiding. That is what often happens."

"You think he is just HIDING?" Ed sounded hopeful. "I was afraid maybe he might be hurt."

"Yes, well, a shock reaction may follow a severe fright. During the war, there were many such cases with cats . . ."

"Shock reaction?" To Ed there was an ominous ring to the words.

113

"Yes. The cat may be hiding out of fear. Sometimes following such a shock, some cats become catatonic."

"What's that?"

"Sort of like playing possum." Dr. Fox tried to sound reassuring. "Sometimes they snap out of it by themselves.

"What can I do?"

"I'm afraid there's nothing you CAN do." Ed was silent.

Dr. Fox went on, "Gentle handling and reassurance often helps . . ."

"But if I can't find him . . ."

"You'll just have to wait. He may recover by himself." Then Dr. Fox said very crisply the thing he had to say to this man. "However, in some cases, the shock reaction is collapse and sudden death."

The phone was dead for an instant. "I see." Ed paused. "Thank you, doctor." Then he put the phone down very carefully.

His secretary came to the doorway, her eyes questioning.

"The vet says we'll just have to wait. He thinks the cat may be in some kind of shock. He'll either recover, or . . . It's up to Mosby."

"He's a strong cat," she said gently. "No little old noise is going to get him down."

"Yeah," said Ed. "He's a tough old boy." She couldn't bear the way her boss's shoulders drooped. She tiptoed out.

And so they waited. Ed couldn't get that awful picture out of his mind. The cat lying hid somewhere, unable to move. Scared to death. That was not just a saying anymore.

*   *   *

It had been a week now. Ed went up every morning with fresh food. He felt so hopeless, but he still went through the ritual of feeding. Ed walked slowly into Mosby's Hideout. His hope was beginning to fade. He looked down at the dish he'd left yesterday. He stared at it, unbelieving. Then suddenly, he found himself grinning from ear to ear. The dish was empty. For some reason, Ed found he couldn't see very clearly. His glasses misted. He blinked and peered around.

"Mosby?" A gray figure emerged from a shadow and crept slowly over toward him. "Hello, fella," he whispered. "Hey, there!" He stooped and held his hand down. The cat hesitated and then rubbed against it, ever so gently. Ed felt his ribs and the tangled fur. He put down the fresh dish and watched as Mosby ate, growling softly.

"I bet you're pretty hungry after all that . . . eh?" Ed cleared his throat. He watched his cat for a long time, still grinning a bit shakily.

"You're a tough old fella, Mosby!" he said.

17

Christmas and a New Start

E d was so relieved to find Mosby had survived the ordeal
of the fireworks, he blotted out the problem he still had
to face: what to do with Mosby? We all know the feeling.
Something unpleasant looms there in the future—but not too
close. Not yet. So we tuck it away in the back of our minds, or
bury it underneath daily chores, hoping it will go away. Knowing it won't. Hoping for a miracle.

Ed decided not to bother Roger with news of the cat's return. Maybe it just slipped his mind. There were so many things
happening—new plays, ballets, concerts, plans for the new theater.

As the winter holidays approached, the Chairman called his
Building Manager to make more plans.

"When the new President takes office in January," he said,
"his inaugural celebration will be held here, at the Kennedy
Center, all on national TV. That evening, the President and his

cabinet, members of Congress and the diplomatic corps, all sorts of VIPs and their families will be here."

"Wow!" said Ed. "We're going to have quite a time! That's going to be some security problem!"

Everyone was busy. There was not much opportunity to worry about one cat.

Suddenly, Christmas was upon them. Even Mosby caught the spirit. Outside, the river was bright and glittery. The balcony sparkled with frost, but as yet there was no snow. Each evening, a bright star hung low over the trees. It shined with a strange brilliance in the afterglow. Little colored lights winked from the buildings on the far shore.

Inside, the halls were decked with boughs of holly. The Kennedy Center echoed with bells, music and laughter. Handel's Hallelujahs rang until the chandeliers danced. Mosby, of course, preferred the ballet. He was enchanted with the Nutcracker! The swirling, dancing—all those children and the toys and the colors. He had never seen a nursery or a toy, but somehow he was drawn by the warmth of the scene far below him. He yowled right along with the music.

One night, when he went back through the hole to his nighttime spot, he was surprised and delighted. The A.F.I. offices were aglow. A small, green tree stood by the water cooler. Tiny bulbs winked in its branches. They lit up silver streamers, little balls and figures. Now a dog would hardly notice such a tree. But to a cat, this was irresistible.

Mosby went up close. He sniffed. A sharp scent, new to him, tickled his nose. He patted one ball carefully. He noticed his small, distorted reflection in it. Soon he grew bolder, hitting at the balls high and low. One fell off and rolled under the water cooler. It was quite a game to reach it. He dribbled it, soccer-fashion, paw to paw, the length of the long carpet and back, where it crashed into the mirror and broke. He glared at his other self, as if it was HIS fault. He hooked another ball off the

"He patted one ball carefully, noticing his small distorted reflection
in it."

tree and invented his own circus act by lying on his back and balancing the ball in his paws.

As he rolled over, a pungent aroma rose from a small package under the tree. He sniffed at it, then with swift claws tore off the paper. It was Christmas Eve. Someone had left him a present. It was a cloth mouse. It smelled like nothing he had ever smelled. Oh, so delicious! He felt positively kittenish. He tossed the toy mouse in the air. He rolled over and over with it. And when he finally went to sleep under his plant, he guarded his present with one paw.

Mosby liked Christmas!

*   *   *

One January day, Ed's secretary said, "Ceci sent around Mosby's monthly supply. That cat must be enormous by now, the amount of food he puts away . . ."

Ed didn't look up or smile at her old joke. "We won't be needing it much longer," he said glumly, drawing a doodle of a box with a cat in one corner.

"You mean they are finally going to build the new theater?"

"Yes. They start work next week." Ed drew a large black cloud crowding down on the cat. "Cats have an extra sense," he mused. "Dr. Fox says they can feel a change coming." He looked up at his secretary and almost smiled. "Once, when we moved, we had the car all packed, everyone ready to go, and our cat disappeared. We looked everywhere. Found him in the cellar, glaring at us. Some cats just don't like change. You know, when they start . . . all those workmen . . . the racket . . . I don't know what he'll do . . ."

The secretary said nothing. There really was no answer.

The week passed all too quickly. Early Monday morning, men tromped into Mosby's Hideout, strangers with strange tools. They scuffled about all over his territory, measuring, calling out in

120

loud voices, tapping, thumping, stirring up the dust. They even climbed up to his ledge and left it smelling of cigars. They stayed all day. When they left, Mosby came out of hiding, crouching low, his ears flat. He listened. All was still. They were gone. Only the smell of them lingered in the air.

Ed came in the next day while it was still quite dark, his hands smelling of the cold. This particular morning, he waited around while Mosby finished eating and talked quietly. "You're a lucky son of a gun," Ed said affectionately. "It's cold out there, fella, but you wouldn't know about that." Ed rubbed his hands together. "Whew, that traffic is a mess. The inauguration today has every-thing in a mess. And with the President's party here tonight . . . I've got no business dawdling around." Ed sighed. "Sometimes I wish I could just go back home to Washington State . . ." Ed studied the glossy back bent over the dish. "But then what would become of you?"

Mosby looked up at the sound of the familiar voice and chirped. There was something in the voice . . . something. "What WILL be-come of you, fella!" Ed put down his hand. Mosby rubbed against it, then sat down nearby and started to wash. "They may have both-ered you a little yesterday, but they start work in here in earnest to-morrow . . . Oh, if only you would let me pick you up . . . but I just don't dare. I scared you once. You might never come to me again."

This was the last time Ed ever saw Mosby. He didn't know it was good-bye. It often happens like that, and sometimes, it is best for us not to know. Ed just went off. It was going to be a busy day— what with the Secret Service coming to secure the building and all. The Secret Service people have to make sure there are no suspicious characters around—or anything dangerous, like a bomb, that might hurt the President.

When the Secret Service men came later that morning, Ed tagged along with them. As they entered the door into Mosby's place, one of the men said, "Wow! This is some room! What IS it?"

"It's going to be a little theater . . ."

121

"Little!"

"Yes," said Ed, pushing Mosby's dish further into a dark corner with his foot. "We're about to finish it." He watched the agents poking about. He knew Mosby was watching, too, from some secret hidey-hole. "Well," said Ed, finally, "I've got to get back to work. You know the way down . . ." The men kept on looking in every vent, every corner. They stayed a long time. It made Mosby uneasy. He hid in one of the vents all day. First the noisy workmen, now these silent, secretive men . . .

Toward nightfall, he heard sounds of a party, and circling around the people near the fire doors, he slipped into his secret passage to see what was up. All the noise and confusion had made him hungry. There were a lot of people milling around. What a feast they were setting out! Finally everyone left. Then he sneaked out—no waiters, no Henri showed up. So he made a nice meal of turkey, right there on the floor of the banquet hall. Everyone seemed to have gone off to watch some kind of big doings.

When he went back to his Hideout, a man was standing in the middle of his floor. Just standing there. Mosby could barely make him out in the darkness. There was another by the door to the elevator, another at the door to the A.F.I. offices. Mosby tried to sneak up to his ledge, but one of the men spotted him.

"Hey, what's that?" The voice was sharp. Mosby ran toward the hole under the door to the offices, but there was a man standing in the middle of the carpet by his plant. A voice behind him shouted, "Here's a cat. What's a cat doing here?" Someone tried to grab him.

Mosby panicked. The fire door was open. He scurried through it and down some stairs. At every landing there was another man. So Mosby kept going, down and down. All of a sudden, he was outside the building. The cold air hit him like a blow. He didn't know it could be this cold. He was breathing fast. The icy air hurt his throat. Ahead of him was a long line of black cars, engines humming. They looked tremendous to Mosby, who had only seen cars far off on the bridges.

There were footsteps behind him. Mosby found himself looking into the open door of one of the big cars. Without even thinking, he leapt in. He heard voices approaching and crawled quickly into the folds of a lap robe hanging behind the front seat. It was warm and dark there, and he stayed very still as some people got into the car and settled into the back seat.

The car door shut behind them. The first voice Mosby heard was small and wistful.

"Now can I put my glasses on?"

"Yes, dear." This was the voice of an older woman. "It's all right now. We just wanted you to look your prettiest for the party."

"Don't you like my glasses?"

"I love your glasses."

Mosby hunched forward until he could just see a little girl leaning back in a corner of the wide seat. Mosby liked her looks. The glasses reminded him of Ed. He ducked back into the robe.

"Boy," said the girl, "I'm tired. I'm glad I don't have to stay to the end like Mom and Dad."

"Don't worry, dear, we'll be home soon."

"Home!" Mosby heard a big yawn and yawned himself. "That big, old White House? It . . . it's just not cozy. You could get lost in there."

"Well, dear, it's your home for now."

"Yeah, I guess. But I don't like it—all those long halls and shiny rooms. It's just too big and . . . er . . . elegant!"

"I know. You are a good, brave little girl. Remember, we're not going to be there forever."

"I miss my friends. I wish I had someone . . . something . . . you know, sometimes I just get . . . lonely . . ." The voice trailed off. There was a deep sigh.

123

"He could just see a little girl leaning back in the seat."

Mosby heard someone get in the front seat. A door slammed. "Sh!" said the woman, leaning forward toward the driver. "She's asleep. The President said you should take us home and come back for him and the First Lady later."

Mosby felt the engine start. The lap robe, like a hammock, rocked him gently as the car swung around and up the ramp to the parkway.

What did she say? A great big house to get lost in . . . lots of parties. That didn't sound too bad! Of course, it wouldn't be the Kennedy Center. But when you have to move, you can't be too choosy. Besides, these people and this new life might prove quite interesting . . .

In the days that followed, Ed looked hard for Mosby. He searched all over the empty theater. He asked around everywhere in the Kennedy Center. He even inquired at nearby buildings.

"Well," he said to his secretary one day, "I give up. He's gone for good."

The secretary tried to see the bright side. "He certainly solved your problem for you. I mean, what to do with him. You said he might disappear. I'll bet he found a good place to stay."

"Yes," said Ed. "Not just any place would do. I'm going to miss that fella. He was quite a cat."

*   *   *

Well, that's the story of Mosby. He was big, he was gray and maybe not so wild as he thought. It is a true story—all except, perhaps, the last part. He did disappear that night of the presidential inaugural, but no one knows for sure where he went when he left.

All things considered, I rather think he might have ended up in that big, "elegant" house. For a cat like Mosby, as Ed put it, not just ANY place would do.